# Truth and Salsa

# Truth and Salsa

## LINDA LOWERY

PEACHTREE
ATLANTA

Ω
Published by
PEACHTREE PUBLISHERS
1700 Chattahoochee Avenue
Atlanta, Georgia 30318-2112

*www.peachtree-online.com*

Cover design by Loraine M. Joyner
Book design by Melanie McMahon Ives

Printed in the United States of America
10 9 8 7 6 5 4 3 2 1
First Edition

Library of Congress Cataloging-in-Publication Data

Keep, Linda Lowery.
    Truth and salsa / by Linda Lowery. -- 1st ed.
        p. cm.
    Summary: Having moved temporarily from Michigan to live with her
grandmother in Mexico, twelve-year-old Hayley tries to sort out her
feelings about her parents' separation while also helping some
townsmen who have run into trouble while working in the United States.
    ISBN 1-56145-366-8
    [1. Family problems--Fiction.  2. Fathers--Fiction.  3. Grandmothers
--Fiction.  4. Migrant labor--Fiction.  5. Ghosts--Fiction.  6. Mexico
--Fiction.]      I. Title.
PZ7.K25115Tru 2006
[Fic]--dc22
                                                        2005027633

*For* los niños *who still wait for Dad...*

—L. L.

# Contents

# 1

## Adiós, Kalamazoo!

I'd like to tell you I have silky caramel skin, my eyes
are dark as the night sky, and my shiny raven hair
touches my waist when I brush it out. But that would
be a lie. And besides, would that make me sound cooler
than I really am? Someday you might meet me and you'd
be all disappointed, and you'd never believe another word
that came out of my big mouth.

It's like what people do when they date on the Internet.
They make stuff up, like they're tall and blonde and love
to sail. Then they never want to meet the other person
face-to-face because if they did, the truth would come out.
My guess is that a lot of them miss hooking up with their
soul mates because they're too chicken to be honest about
who they are, warts and all.

So here's the truth: I have tons of freckles and my skin
is so white it practically glows in the dark. My curly hair
is a natural shade of squirrel—not really brown, not really
red. My eyes are green. So I figure I won't exactly blend in
when I get to Mexico.

My dad would probably be happy about that. He thinks
I'm going from normal, respectable Michigan to a place so

backward they don't even speak English. So third-world they've probably never heard of e-mail or iPods or even vacuum cleaners.

Actually I don't really know what my dad would think, since he hardly ever calls anyway. I just remember what he said about Gran when she left for Mexico. I can still hear him now: "Mexico? You'll stick out like a red, white, and blue thumb."

I'm thinking of tweaking my name just a smidge to help me fit in a little better. How does this sound? "My name is..." Wait, excuse me, let's try this in Spanish. *"Me llamo Margarita Flynn."* Other than the Flynn, I 'd say it works great.

My parents named me Hayley Margaret. My middle name is in honor of my dad's mom, who died before I was born. Frankly I'm liking the sound of Margarita. Worldly. Sophisticated. Romantic, don't you think? Margarita means "daisy." The name Hayley just does not translate, not even in Spanish class, which is where I got the idea to switch to Margarita in the first place.

Anyway, I'm sure if I tried my new name out on my dad, he'd give me one of his I'm-not-impressed grunts. But he doesn't get a say when he hasn't even offered for me to go live with him for a while. I'm baggage, and he wants to travel unencumbered, I guess.

Here's the deal: back in April, Dad split. Disappeared in our Lexus—oops, *his* Lexus—with nothing but his laptop and cell phone and the twenty-eight perfectly pressed suits from his closet. He left a message on the answering machine about how my mom had better figure out a serious way to get some help and how he had to go live his own life. And oh yeah: "Hayley, take care of your mother."

I tried to do that. But I guess I'm not very good at it. Three months have passed since then, and things have not gotten better. Mom has a problem with me going to Mexico, too. She thinks it's all her fault I have to go off to some faraway country where I can't even drink the water.

The truth about my mom is hard to put into words. My stomach turns into a huge empty hole every time I start. I mean, I'm usually very open and talkative, but some things sit way down inside you and need time before they're ready to come out as words. If you don't mind, I'd rather not talk about the whole Mom thing right now.

Anyway, I'm secretly very excited about this Mexico adventure, except for one thing: I have no idea how I'm going to survive without my friends, especially Samantha. She's the only one who knows me inside out and upside down. We've been seeing each other twelve hours every day to make up for the 4,383 hours I'll be gone, which is the number of hours I figured out there are in six months.

Sam's been helping me cram anything and everything I can fit into the two-suitcase maximum the airline allows. I'm bringing pictures of my friends, my favorite books, my Spanish dictionary, and Farley, my beat-up teddy frog. I packed my paints and brushes, too. Sam gave me some rolled-up canvases to take with me. That's because Ms. Stucky, our art teacher, told us the art canvas in Mexico smells like horse glue. Nice.

But clothes? I have no idea.

"What do people wear down there?" I asked Gran on the

phone. Gran's been living in Mexico for three years—she just upped and moved one September. We've never visited her there because my father thinks she's lost her marbles. She does come back to stay with us every Christmas, and I have to say, after careful consideration, I don't think she's at all crazy. Just...quirky.

"People wear whatever they want," Gran told me. That was not enough information. So I tried Sam, since she's Mexican American.

"Do you think the girls wear long skirts with lacy blouses?" I ask. That could be fun, with my freckly shoulders peeking out over frilly white lace.

"Probably," Sam says.

A big help she is.

Has she ever been to Mexico? No.

Does she speak Spanish? *No mucho.* She picked French even though I begged her to be in Spanish class with me.

Does she want to come with me to keep her best friend company? She does, but she can't.

*¡Qué lástima!* What a shame!

It's not that I don't want to go. I do. I'm excited that *me llamo* Margarita, and I can't wait to be with Gran in Mexico.

But once in a while when I'm lying in bed alone, that big empty black hole starts opening up inside me again. Which means I'm already missing Mom.

# 2
## Moose Tracks

It all started with a letter from Gran telling me how beautiful Mexico is. Inside the envelope was a little silvery heart, like a charm for a bracelet. I didn't know it meant anything until she called a few weeks later. It was exactly June 19, as a matter of fact. Just after school got out. I was heading to the Dairy Berry for a Moose Tracks sundae with Sam.

"How about you come live with me for a while, so your mom can take a bit of time to deal with her problems?" asked Gran.

What? In Mexico?

"Thanks, Gran, but I don't think so," I told her. "I have a lot going on." Actually I didn't have much at all going on besides having a lazy and wonderful summer. But my mom needed me. Since Dad left, she'd been having a hard time getting on with her life.

Sorry...that's not the whole truth.

The real truth? My mother is broken. She's like a house whose windows got shattered by flying bricks. Now cold air whips right through, freezing the warm corners inside.

Then Gran explained that my mom needed to go away for a while, like for *six months,* to a depression treatment center in Denver. I felt the phone freeze in my hand. I looked across the table at my mom, who was sitting there clutching her fingers tight, gazing at me wide-eyed like a deer stunned by headlights. She's going into some loony bin? *My* mom? I wanted to hang up, but I couldn't move.

"It'll be very good for your mom," Gran chirped. "And for you, too, Hayley Cakes."

She went on about how hard it'd been for Mom and me, and how healing this place was supposed to be, that Mom'd be fit as a fiddle before too long. I held the phone away from my ear and stared at my mom.

"Why didn't you tell me?" I asked her. I could tell that my voice sounded hurt and scared and mad all at the same time. What I really wanted to say was: "How come you're sitting right here and somebody needs to call from *Mexico* to tell me what's going on?" But Mom is so fragile, I have to be careful about words that just pop out.

"So we think it's a good idea for you to stay with me for a while. We'll get to know each other in a whole new way," I heard Gran saying. "It'll be fun."

*Stop!* I wanted to shout. First of all, I felt like a Ping-Pong ball. Gran on the phone. Mom at the table. Me bouncing from one to the other in the middle.

Second, I had a bunch of questions.

Why was I the one who had to turn my whole life topsy-turvy when none of this was my fault? How did all this happen without anybody asking me?

I could *not* go to Mexico. I had to change their minds. I

tried the only leverage I could think of at the moment:

"Can't I stay with Dad?" I asked, even though I already knew the answer. No. I'm part of all the stuff he left behind so he wouldn't be encumbered, remember? There was a weird silence and then Gran sighed a deep sigh.

"I'm afraid not, sugar. Your dad's not exactly acting like Father of the Year these days. To tell you the truth, I'd like to march into his fancy-pants office and wring his darn neck."

I tried another tactic.

"What about school?" I asked.

"They have schools in Mexico, for heaven's sake," said Gran. "You can really work on your art here. You can study Spanish, or guitar, or whatever else floats your boat."

"It will give me time to get my act together, sweetie," whispered my mom. She had a tremble in her voice.

I couldn't believe this was really going to happen. Obviously everyone had talked this whole plan over and it was already carved in stone. There was nothing I could do about it.

"Fine," I said. "Whatever." It wasn't really fine at all. "I'll talk to you tomorrow, Gran."

I hung up. I had to get out of there. Get some air. Get some ice cream.

"Sam's waiting for me," I told my mom. "I've got to go."

When I got back, I was feeling a little calmer since I'd gotten a chance to cry into my sundae about leaving for six months. Sam cried, too. A best friend is somebody you can sob into your Moose Tracks with.

Mom was still at the table, but now she had the atlas open to Mexico.

"You might really like Mexico, honey," she said. "It's sunny."

Hmmm...I tried to switch gears for Mom's sake, like I learned when Mom and I went to therapy together so I could understand what was happening with her and me when Dad left us. There are at least two truths to every situation. Sometimes you have to force yourself to look at the positive side, no matter how hard that might be.

It took a minute, but soon I conjured up a rosy picture of me in Mexico: My toes were wiggling at the edge of the ocean, a gauzy white top floating over my teeny tropical bikini.

"Gran lives here, in a town called San Miguel de Allende," Mom told me, pointing on the map. She was pointing far from the ocean, to the very middle of Mexico. "It's in the Sierra Madre Mountains."

Huh? Wait just a sec here. I was moving to a dot in the middle of a foreign country, where we'd already established that they speak a different language, and now it's *hundreds of miles* from a beach?

My dreamy bikini scene came crashing down around me, and reality thunked like a boulder into the pit of my stomach. My image switched to what was probably closer to the truth about San Miguel: There was one dusty road down the middle of a town lined with those Mexican bars they call *cantinas*. And burros delivered the mail. Several days late.

"It will be an adventure, honey," said Mom. Her eyes were pleading, *forgive me*. "It's just for six months."

8

Six months! Didn't she know that six months away from Kalamazoo, from my friends, from my school, was f...o...r...e...v...e...r?

But I made myself get up and give Mom the biggest hug I could muster. Her body felt as fragile as a fawn's. I just wished I could make her happy.

# 3
# Rapunzel's Tower

July came up a lot quicker than I ever expected, and I said *adiós* to America the Beautiful. I was nervous about going through customs, where my dad says they rip through all your clothes and books to see if you're sneaking in illegal stuff. So Gran met me in the airport in Dallas wearing a turquoise dress with a hot pink shawl and big, dangly earrings.

We flew to Mexico City together and customs turned out to be nothing. The officials gave us a green light, so we walked right through without my bags being unzipped. The moon was full and white when—two buses and one taxi later—Gran and I finally arrived in San Miguel.

"Welcome to my little house—our *casita*," Gran announces proudly as we get out of the taxi. We climb some rock stairs and open a bright blue wooden door arched at the top. There's an orange cactus pot on the stoop and a long cobblestone path leading into a humongous garden filled with plants way taller than me. Tin lanterns on the trees are shaped like masks, with glowing turquoise marbles for eyes. There are holes punched in the metal and twinkly light flickers through.

"Spooky," I whisper.

"Exotic," says Gran.

Paths of steps snake up to the house, which is built out of big stones and is completely—

"Round?" I blurt out, standing with my mouth hanging open.

"Oh, didn't I tell you I live in a round house? It's my Rapunzel tower," says Gran.

The moonlight is shimmering blue and ghosty on the rocks. Rapunzel's tower, if you recall, was really a fairy-tale prison. We unlock the iron latch on the thick oak doors.

Whoa! The walls inside are all rock, too, and when I drop my bags, I'm staring smack in the face of a life-sized grinning skeleton who is wearing a skirt.

I let out a scream. (Just so you know, I'm a screamer. It used to drive my dad insane.)

"What's *that?*" I yell, backing off and taking my pseudo-karate stance.

"Oh, that's Cynthia," Gran says casually. "Papier-mâché. She's fun, isn't she?" Cynthia dangles from a rafter, her paper bones clattering softly in the breeze. Gulp.

Gran flips a switch and dim lights beam up from the floor along the walls. There are little crannies holding candles and nooks with tiny framed pictures of saints inside.

For just a second I think of my dad saying how crazy Gran is, but I erase that thought pronto. I'm not going to let my brain start fantasizing that I'm stuck in a round house in a Mexican jungle with a crazy grandma I don't know that well.

11

Ducking to avoid a collision with Cynthia's bony feet, I follow Gran up a spiral staircase. I'm jittery. I don't know what I expected, but it sure wasn't what I'm seeing now. There are savage-looking masks staring from every wall, some with snakes and toads on their heads.

I breathe a sigh of relief as we wind past Gran's bedroom with the four-poster bed I remember from when I was little. And her library, which has a cozy sitting area with Gran's old Victorian reading lamp.

The next floor at the tippy-top is like an observatory. Most of the room is windows, with skylights in the ceiling. I look at the stars twinkling above and the town twinkling below.

"See over there? That's the *Parroquia* in the main square," chirps Gran, pointing. The moon is floating over a big pink church with spires and lots of lights.

"Doesn't it look like Sleeping Beauty's castle in the moonlight?" asks Gran.

I can tell she's overjoyed to show me all these things she loves. My mind jumps to another unfortunate comparison. We all know the wicked fairy cast a spell on the poor sleeping princess that laid her flat for a hundred years.

"To me it looks like a birthday cake, all lit up," I suggest. I didn't know I'd feel so weird being in a new place. Am I having culture shock? Everything is strange, like I'm barefoot in the snow, or wearing boots on the beach. It's just...*off,* somehow.

We'd told Mom we'd give her a buzz in the morning to let her know I arrived safe and sound. I kind of want to call her right now. But I don't want to be a baby. After all,

I'm practically thirteen. Instead I plop onto the bed and sink into a pale yellow comforter and nice, soft pillows.

"Very homey," I say, snuggling in deeper.

"Good, because this is your room," says Gran. "It's perfect for you, full of starlight."

"Great," I say. Rapunzel's penthouse is all mine.

"Your bathroom is over there, and I left a flashlight on the bedside table in case the lights go out. We have electrical problems sometimes."

Not good. I look over to make sure I know exactly where that flashlight is. Beside it I see a vase chock-full of pink roses.

"Welcome to Mexico," Gran says, smiling. "I wanted you to have everything you need, and some flowers to boot."

"*Gracias,* Gran," I say, leaning over for a sweet sniff.

"Now, *buenas noches, tesoro,*" she says.

I know *buenas noches* means good night. "What's *tesoro?*" I ask.

"Treasure," Gran says sweetly, pinching my cheek. She gives me a little goodnight kiss on my forehead. "You're my treasure, and I'm so glad you're here."

When Gran leaves I dig into my suitcase for a comfy sweatshirt and lie back down on the bed with Farley in my arms.

Down the hillside the night is hopping. Sounds from the town are floating up and right into my tower. I hear people speaking in Spanish. Laughter. *Mariachis* singing. Guitar music. Church bells ringing the hour.

It all sounds nice, but everything here is so new to me. I'm more comfortable with the crickets and car engines and tunes from the radio that put me to sleep in Kalamazoo.

"What did we get ourselves into?" I whisper to Farley, hugging him closer.

I don't know what I'm feeling right now. Happy and sad. Excited and afraid. Six months is a very long time. Sam is really, really far away. And my mom... How is she going to make it, first without Dad, and now without me?

I think about her frightened eyes, focused deep inside herself instead of out toward the world. She needs somebody to take good care of her. They'd better be kind and good at that hospital, or center, or whatever you call that place where she is.

I lie motionless for a while, listening to the Mexican night.

After a few minutes my toes are wiggling and my mind is racing. I'm way too restless to sleep. I creep out of bed with Farley, grab the flashlight, and take a little tour of my room. I hang some of my clothes in the huge hand-carved chifforobe. I brush my teeth in the blue and green sink that's painted with calla lilies. Then I decide I could use a shower. While I'm washing my hair, I stand on my tippy toes and peek out the tiny round window rimmed in orange tiles. In the moonlight I can see white chickens and a few goats wandering around in the yard next door.

Pretty soon I'm tiptoeing down the spiral staircase, checking out Gran's library. She has a tall red ladder for reaching the high shelves. There are books and magazines galore. A painted rooster. Plaster skulls. Little silver body parts stuck on picture frames. Mini body parts? What's up with that?

There's so much stuff everywhere, it looks like a Christmas stocking somebody turned inside out.

Farley and I carefully spiral our way down to the first floor. I shine the flashlight over my head and shudder at Cynthia's grinning face. My light runs along the wood beams of the ceiling, which is all strung with papery skull banners. They're fluttering like clothes on a line.

Whoops! I stub my toe on a table shaped like a striped dog. Ouch! Farley goes soaring toward the kitchen. I see a shadowy hand reaching out from behind the kitchen counter.

# 4
# A Midnight Snack

lying frog!" Gran shouts, stretching out her hands to catch Farley. She manages to grab him by the leg. I let out a big sigh of relief.

"What are you doing up so late, Gran?" I ask, turning off the flashlight. I rescue Farley and plop him in a chair. I see Gran has been working on something on the kitchen table under a reading lamp.

Tiny silver arms and legs and kidneys are scattered across the table. Hearts, too, like the one she sent me in Kalamazoo. She sits back down, picks up a little hammer, and starts pounding a body part onto the frame with teeny nails.

"I couldn't sleep, either," she says. "I'm too excited that you're here, I guess. I can't wait to show you everything in Mexico. You'll love it, sweetums."

"Yeah?" I say. I'm not sure. So far it's a little creepy.

"There's hot chocolate on the stove, if you want some," she says, tap-tapping a mini-heart onto the frame. "And check out what's in the cupboards."

Gran's cabinets are jam-packed with chips and cookies and puffy bags of pink and white marshmallows. I feel my heart go soft. I know she bought all this stuff for me. It's been a long time since anybody bought me treats without my even asking.

"I'm looking for a cocoa mug," I tell her.

"To the left, over the sink," she says. I'm used to matching cups lined up in neat rows. Each of Gran's cups is different. I take one that says J' ♥ PARIS. I love Paris.

"Oh, you chose Paris!" Gran says cheerfully when I sit back down. "That's twenty years old, that mug. From a trip with your grandpa to my favorite city on earth."

"What are you doing with that stuff?" I ask, eyeing the scattered body parts on the table.

"Oh, I just enjoy making these frames," she says, tapping a left hand onto the edge.

"They're like the little heart you sent me," I say, picking up a foot. "What exactly are they? Charms?"

"They're *milagros*. Miracles," says Gran, as if she just said they were scrambled eggs or something perfectly ordinary. "You believe in miracles, don't you, *tesoro?*"

Well, sure, I believe in miracles. Or at least I did when I was little. Like Santa. Or Sam calling just when I was picking up the phone to call her. But I'm not sure anymore if those are technically considered miracles.

"I guess," I mumble.

Then Gran explains about *milagros*. Let's say you broke your arm. You buy an arm *milagro* and bring it to church. You pin it to the robe on the statue of a particular saint. That saint will automatically know that your arm needs healing. Then you pray and pray, and soon your arm will feel better.

"I have a hard time believing a statue of a saint can heal you," I say slowly.

"Ah, but that's the *milagro,* the miracle!" says Gran wisely. "I just love the way they look, strewn all over the frames."

Hmmm. I'm not sure I do, so I keep my mouth shut.

"Say, I have something for us to try," says Gran, hopping up.

She pulls what looks like a king-sized orange pillow out of a cabinet. It's actually cheese puffs in a gigantic bag, the size they have in school cafeterias. She plunks it beside the *milagros.* Then she brings a bowl of salsa.

"All the kids eat these," she says. "I waited till you came to try them."

"Only the best for me, huh, Gran?" I tease.

*"Eso es.* You got that right," she quips. We each dip one puff in the salsa and give them a try. The cheese puffs are all air, and the salsa is *picante*—fiery.

"Aargh!" I cry. My eyes start to water like crazy. "All I can taste is the hot sauce!"

"It's my special sweet and spicy mango salsa," Gran says proudly. "Salsa's a little like life, you know? Some people prefer it bland and ordinary. I like it a little more interesting."

Interesting? I grab for my cocoa and take a few gulps.

The cocoa is spicy, too. "And what's in the hot chocolate? It's...cinnamon-y," I gasp.

"It's Mexican chocolate, darlin'. *Abuelita,* it's called. Everybody drinks chocolate with cinnamon here."

"I know what *abuelita* means," I brag. "It means Grandma."

"You saw the picture of that old lady who looks like me right on the package, didn't you?" Gran says.

"No. I learned that word in Spanish class." Now we're having fun, teasing each other. "You look younger than that lady, anyway. And that's the truth."

"Why, thank you, sweetie. I hope so," she says in a high-pitched fake old lady voice.

"So what made you move to Mexico in the first place, *Abuelita?*" I ask. I chomp down on a few more puffs dipped in just a dab of salsa. Gran goes back to her work.

"Oh my. So many things." Pound. Tap-tap. "The fiestas." Tap-tap. "The colors." Tap-tap. "The weather, the butterflies. But mostly the people," she answers, looking up at me over her glasses.

"I don't know much about Mexican people," I admit. "I mean, my friend Samantha is just like me. I don't exactly think of her as Mexican."

"That's because she's not. She's Mexican American, born and raised in the U.S."

"Well, there are all those migrant workers who come to Michigan to pick grapes in summer and fall," I remember. "But I don't really know any of them. We only see them working in the vineyards. Then they go right home to their trailers."

"Of course they do. They're up north to work. They don't have money to go out to movies and restaurants. They send their money back home here to their families."

Gran had a point there. What a hard life.

"You'll learn so much while you're here," Gran continues. "And I've got lots of plans for us."

She tells me about the fiestas. Tap-tap. And all the

beautiful crafts on display in the village square. Tap-tap. And the butterfly forest where millions of monarchs fly down to spend the winter...and the butterfly wings, the butterfly wings sprout from my shoulders and I go soaring over the pink church and somebody starts ruffling my antennae on my curly head...

"Hayley!" I hear a whisper. "Wake up and go to bed now, *tesoro.*"

I jerk my head up off the table. "Did I fall asleep? Sorry, Gran," I mutter, all foggy. Gran pulls a cheese puff off my cheek. It's flat from being slept on. She ties a bright pink ribbon around it.

"Nothing to be sorry for. It's been a long day." She takes out a big nail and pounds it between the rocks in the wall. Then she hangs the puff from the nail. Finally she stands back, admiring the hanging cheese puff like it's a work of art.

Am I dreaming again? No.

"It will remind me of our first night in Mexico together, *tesoro,*" Gran whispers, smiling.

Sweet. And strange. Is it possible Gran's even weirder than me?

# 5

## La Fantasma

Roosters are crowing, ducks are quacking, and bells are clanging when I wake up. What a racket! And where am I, anyway? Oh yeah, no wonder I'm confused. I just spent my first night in Mexico, with cheese puffs and body parts.

I peek out of my huge Rapunzel window that overlooks the garden. Gran's down there chatting with a girl who's about my age. Her skin is the color of taffy apples. Not a freckle to be found. She has a glossy black ponytail tied with turquoise beads, and her jeans are way tight.

I squint to read her T-shirt. The words are English, printed in red: "I See DUMB People."

Does the girl know English? Does she get the joke from the movie?

I saunter down the spiral stairs in my sweatshirt, acting all cool like I don't care if I meet anyone because my life is so jam-packed with thrills that I don't *need* to find friends.

I make my blasé appearance, slouching against the railing halfway down the stairs. The girl flips her shiny ponytail and jogs right over.

"Hi. I am your neighbor, Liliana," she says in English, extending her smooth-as-caramel hand for a shake. "I heard you were coming to San Miguel."

She has bright eyes. Like shiny dark chocolate. And she speaks English! I hop down to shake her hand, but I miss a stair and fall flat on my face on the cement floor. Ouch!

"Graceful," I mutter as Liliana helps me up. She looks confused.

"Graceful?" she asks. "Your name is not Hayley?"

"Well, no, I meant, um..."

"Oh, graceful! I get it, Hayley!" says Liliana, laughing a tinkly bell laugh.

Now I'm the one who's confused, because I was planning to be Margarita and Gran obviously already told her my name is Hayley. "My name is Hayley Margarita," I say, compromising.

"Oh! You have a Spanish name, like your *abuelita*. Beautiful!" says Liliana. Gran winks at me as she heads for the kitchen. So Gran's using her Spanish-version name, too. I'm not the only one with romantic thoughts about fitting in. For a minute I can't even remember what Gran's regular name is. It's Susan. She must be going by Susana.

"Just call me Margarita," I tell Liliana.

"Okay. And you just call me Lili."

"Deal," I agree. We finally shake.

"I was up early squeezing limes from our trees to make *limonada,* limeade," Gran chirps, bringing in two icy glasses. "Very tangy. Perfect for a summer morning."

"Thank you, Señora Susi," Lili tells Gran.

*"Gracias, Abuelita,"* I say.

22

"Can you tell that Lili speaks the best English in the neighborhood?" asks Gran.

"Where did you learn it?" I ask Lili.

"Some in my school, but mostly from my papa. He works in the States a lot," she answers.

"He does? Where?" I wonder if he's a grape-picker in Michigan.

"Mostly in Colorado. He picks corn and pumpkins when he is up there."

I'm thinking how I never pictured the grape-pickers in Michigan as dads before, with kids back home. Especially cute kids like Lili with her ironed jeans and excellent English.

"Why don't you girls take your drinks out to the garden and get acquainted?" Gran suggests. "I want to make tortilla soup for dinner before it gets too hot outside."

I never heard of tortilla soup. Sounds like soppy tortillas boiled in water, but I'm not even going there.

Lili and I head out to Gran's private jungle. I watch my feet so I don't catch a toe on the cobblestones. I seem to have developed a klutz problem since I've arrived here. I don't need any more black and blue marks.

I'm glad to say that the garden looks cheerier in the daytime—no spookiness. There are huge twisted cacti that look like old men with whiskers. A single leaf from some of these plants could cover Adam and Eve's whole bodies, and the leaves have fancy veins zigzagging through that I'd like to draw. There's also a chicken coop without the chickens. Hmmm...is it big enough to turn into an art studio? I wonder.

Lili names the trees for me: two limes, one lemon, six

avocados, two bananas, and a ton of ten-foot-tall poinsettias that will bloom, she says, at Christmas. There are fruits I can barely pronounce and can't wait to try when they're ready: *mamey, guayaba, zapote.*

Everywhere I step I feel like I'm inside a Mexican painting. Lili and I sip our frosty green *limonadas* on the bright blue bench by the fountain. Heavy branches of magenta and orange flowers frame our heads. A yellow butterfly flits by. Colorful, huh?

"So...did you see *la fantasma* last night?" Lili asks, shaking me out of my thoughts.

"The what?" I ask. My Spanish seems to have deserted me.

"*La fantasma.* People say your house is...¿*Como se dice?*" Lili makes an O with her mouth and flutters her hands, charades-style.

At first I guess that she's a butterfly, which makes her break down laughing. Then she makes a creepy moaning sound.

"You mean a *ghost?*" I ask.

"Yes." She nods. "A ghost."

There's a ghost in this house? In *Gran's* house?

"Someone died here a few years ago. They say the house is hunted." She doesn't say it all creepy, like she's trying to scare the pants off the new *gringa* on the block. I think she's just curious.

"Haunted," I correct. "Not hunted. Haunted."

"Haunted," Lili repeats. "Hasn't your grandmother told you anything?"

"Um, no...Not about a ghost, anyway," I say. A mix of

fear and excitement is snaking around inside me. "Have you ever seen her? Him? The ghost, I mean?" I ask.

Lili shakes her head. "I have only heard stories," she says. Then she shuts up.

I start to squirm. "Well, tell me about the stories!" I blurt out finally.

I guess Lili was waiting for her cue, because she launches into a long, involved story.

In a nutshell, a very sad *señor* came to live in our house years ago. He never talked to anyone at all, just lived like a hermit. Nobody knows who he was or where he came from. He died one night four years ago.

"In *marzo,* March," says Lili. "I remember, because when we watched his body being carried out, the whole town was purple with jacaranda blossoms."

More on the story: Right before the *señor* died, a *señora* came to live with him. Maybe a friend. Maybe his wife. Maybe a housekeeper. Anyway, after the man died, no one ever saw the *señora* again. There are people who think she died also. Nobody knows for sure. The house sat empty for a long time. Then a few years later, it was rented to a young woman.

"Her name was Angela and she stayed only a few nights," says Lili, dropping her voice. "She was visited by a ghost."

"How do you know?" I ask. The hairs along my arms and neck are tingling.

"My mother saw her on the street when she was leaving. The girl was not hurt, but she was shaking from fear."

"So did the ghost talk to her, or what?" I ask.

"No. What happened was that Angela felt a...presence in the house all evening. When dark came, she was sure it was a ghost on the top floor."

Rapunzel's penthouse? I wonder. As in *my* room?

"Here's the very strange part," Lili goes on, leaning toward me. "Angela started to run down the spiral stairs and fell. As if she had been pushed from behind. She told everyone it was the dead *señor* who pushed her."

"What? Ghosts throw people down the stairs?" I ask. This sounds slightly preposterous.

*"No sé.* I don't know," says Lili, shrugging. "But that is the story people tell."

"Hmmm," I murmur. I'm wondering if anybody's told Gran about this. A resident ghost? I don't like this one bit.

"I just wondered if you had seen anything," Lili says, shrugging. "Or heard anything."

"N-no," I stammer. But then again, I had fallen asleep on the kitchen table. I was so tired when I got back to bed, I passed out as soon my head hit the pillow.

Just as I'm about to ask more questions, somebody calls for Lili from across the neighbor's wall. "It's my mother," says Lili. She quickly gets up and hands me her glass.

"I want to know more about this ghost," I tell her. "Can you come back later?"

"Not today. I have a lot of chores, Margarita," says Lili. "But let's walk down to the *Jardín* tomorrow afternoon," she suggests. I must look confused, so she explains that *jardín,* pronounced har-deen, means "garden."

"The *Jardín* is what we call the big plaza in the center of town, in front of the church," Lili explains. "The town square, I think you say."

"Yes, town square," I agree. "Sure, I'll go. What time?"

"Come to my house around seven or eight," she says.

Hadn't Lili said afternoon? Is eight P.M. afternoon in Mexico? But I don't want to confuse things. I just want to hear more about this ghost.

"Great! I'll be there. *Hasta mañana,*" I tell Lili. "See ya tomorrow."

Lili hurries off and I pop back into the *casita*. Gran is way up the spiral steps, hammering on a stair. I go halfway up and sit on a step.

"Do you know anything about a ghost in this house, Gran?" I ask between her hammer whacks.

"Ghost?" she says, her hammer in midair. "Hmmph. Don't listen to all that, *tesoro*. When it comes down to it, we *all* have ghosts."

"What the heck does that mean?" I ask as I stare into Cynthia's glittering pink eyes. But Gran is preoccupied.

"This stair is loose again," she gripes. "Somebody could trip and go crashing right down and break their bumpus!"

Oh no. My mind starts clicking. Did Angela trip and fall because of the loose stair? Or did the stair get loose because she caught her foot on it when *la fantasma* gave her a shove?

And what about all this klutziness since I arrived—all of my falling and tripping? Maybe it's not just me. It could be a *fantasma*.

I trot into the kitchen to grab a handful of cheese puffs for breakfast. I guess they're growing on me.

As I crunch, I'm thinking that since Lili's English is so good, she knows perfectly well what her T-shirt says about DUMB people. Does she also see DEAD people?

27

# 6
# Chicken Sanctuary

D ump those feathers here in the compost," Gran calls as she piles leaves and twigs in a corner of the garden.

I'm cleaning out the chicken cage to turn it into my private art studio, and I'm sneezing up a storm from all the dust and feathers in the air. One by one I haul over ten bags of chicken yuck and plunk them on Gran's precious compost pile.

She calls it black gold.

I call it manure.

It's noon now on my first whole day in Mexico, and I can't stop thinking about that ghost. I rummage through the woodshed for a rake and shovel and broom. Does the ghost hang out in the woodshed? Does he or she ever fly on this broom at midnight? Whoops, wait…Ghosts don't need brooms. They fly naturally.

I throw gallons of bleach on the chickens' floor and screened walls. Then I hose everything down. I figure if this is by any chance a place *la fantasma* likes to hang out, I'm getting rid of anything familiar. Maybe my cleaning will make it uncomfortable enough that the ghost will want to move on.

I spread out garbage bags on the ground of the coop and plop a couple of straw rugs on top. The boxes in which the chickens laid eggs are the perfect size for my paints and brushes. Now I'm excited. My studio is starting to take shape.

Gran walks by with a shovel full of her black gold.

"Raid the house if you need anything!" she calls. "We've got plenty of stuff you might want that we're not using. Check my study and the back room."

"Thanks!" I holler back. I go inside and grab a calendar, an extra table, and two painted wood chairs from Gran's study. But before I put the furniture in my new studio, I wash it down really well. I mean, what if these are the chairs the ghost sits in at night when we're sleeping? What if *la fantasma* eats at this table? Do ghosts eat? I don't think so, but then again, what *do* I know about ghosts?

Not a whole lot. They're transparent and milky white. They fly around at night scaring people and maybe moving furniture. They make hollow moaning sounds, right?

Although if you think about it, that one ghost in Charles Dickens's *A Christmas Carol* had a whole see-through body, face and clothes and all, and he dragged chains. You could hear him clanking his way from room to room. Creepy.

Some people say you can tell where a ghost is if there's a spot that's always especially cold. Or they say you can smell certain ghosts. They leave behind a scent of flowers or—

"Amazing!" Gran proclaims.

I shriek and leap about ten feet in the air. Clearly my ghost ponderings have made me slightly jumpy.

"My goodness!" says Gran. "I didn't mean to scare you."

"It's okay, Gran," I say sheepishly.

But she's looking around her at my new studio. "It's a sanctuary," she says. "Just like a butterfly needs a chrysalis, every person needs a sanctuary."

She's right about that. I'm going to hang a sign on the door, but I don't know what it should say yet. "Keep Out"? *"Fantasmas* Knock Twice"?

"Do you want a computer in there?" Gran asks.

"Sure," I say.

"There's one up in my bedroom closet," Gran says. "It was here when I bought the house, and I've never used it. I'm not exactly the computer type."

Wow, this is great! My dad would no sooner let me put a computer in a chicken coop than dye my hair green. Gran is so laid back.

I run upstairs to take a shower and rinse off the chicken ick. As I'm soaping up, I stand on my tiptoes to peek out the tiny round window again. In the daylight it's busy over at our neighbor's—not Lili's house, the one on the other side.

I can see a lady, dressed not exactly fashionably. She's wearing a ratty purple sweater, a red skirt, pink flip-flops, and a jumbo pair of men's gloves. There's a flowered scarf over her head. She's tossing corncobs to two big pigs in her yard. There are goats, dogs, cats, chickens, a rooster, and a dirty green pond with ducks swimming in it. We've got a whole zoo next door!

After my shower I haul out the computer. It has a printer and a monitor and all the cords. But before I set up, Gran and I take a tortilla soup break. It's not at all like the goop I pictured. She said she started out with a thin tomato soup, then added bits of chicken and avocado and cheese and crispy tortilla chips. Yum!

"Maybe you can teach me how to e-mail awful jokes to my friends on that computer one of these days," says Gran, plopping a spoonful of sour cream on her soup.

"You need the Internet for that, Gran," I explain. "You don't have it here in San Miguel, right?"

Gran frowns. "Of course we do. That's why they call it the World Wide Web. I'm the one who's behind the times. I'll tell you what. If you promise to teach me e-mail, I'll have the Internet hooked up this week."

"Deal," I say happily.

"Okeydoke! And say, after we eat, let's call your mom," Gran adds. "Your dad, too, if you want."

No need to call my dad. I'll get his answering machine because he'll be in a meeting. He's always in a meeting. But I call Mom, and she sounds a slight bit cheerier already. She's leaving for her "center" tomorrow morning, and she's feeling hopeful about everything. Her optimism gives me the tiniest spark of hope, too.

Maybe I should pray for a Mom *milagro,* I think as I head back to my chicken sanctuary. I'm not sure what body part that calls for. A head? A heart?

I run a thick orange extension cord out of the house and into my coop. I set up the computer on my table, plug everything in, and flip the On switch.

Then it dawns on me. It was here when Gran moved in.

Which means this is the ghost's computer. A chill starts creeping along my arms and neck.

I'm waiting, waiting for something to pop up on the screen. I see the computer is registered to "Veronica." Who's Veronica? The mysterious *señora* who was here when the *señor* died? Or is she *la fantasma?* The screen starts filling up with little icons. Should I try going into Veronica's Word program?

I know curiosity killed the cat. But I guess I was just born curious.

Click!

No dice. I try to open pictures and documents and everything else I can find. They're all blank, and the names of the documents are gobbledy-gook.

*Nada.* Zip.

Oh well.

Wait a minute! I see something else. The trash bin is full—the garbage icon shows little sheets of paper stuffed inside.

I click on View Recycle Bin. A couple of icons pop onto the screen. My heart just about stops. Ohmigosh! I can't breathe.

I'm staring at a file called *Privada.* Private.

Private notes? From the ghost?

Click.

More files pop up, labeled in Spanish. They're all dates: 10 *enero,* 25 *febrero,* 14 *marzo*—a bunch of files, about twenty-five of them, dated from January to March, with no year listed. Didn't Lili say the man died in March? Are these things he wrote before he died?

My mind is racing 150 miles per hour. Do I have a right to open these files? Is it even legal? Gran said it's her computer now. But...would I want somebody reading my personal notes after I'm dead and gone?

Absolutely, positively, *definitely* not.

In fact, I'm making a mental note right this minute. Get rid of anything *privada* I've left on my computer as soon as I get back to Kalamazoo. And anything I've written in my sketchbooks, which is where I not only draw, but write down thoughts as well.

I jump up and pace around my chicken coop. I feel like a cartoon character with an angel on one shoulder and a devil on the other.

My devil says: "Do it. You're probably doing the ghost a favor by reading these files. Then you can delete them if you find bad things."

My angel says: "Not so fast, *amiga*. Notice that jumpy feeling in your stomach? You're snooping where you don't belong."

My devil: "Better you than some blabby gossip finding these files. Besides, they may be nothing."

My angel: "Push that Delete button, young lady, and get busy painting something, which is why you cleaned up this chicken coop in the first place."

Pace, pace, pace. Devil. Angel. Devil. Angel. I sit back down. I rub my hands together. I take a deep breath.

Then I click on Open File.

# 7
# The V. Files

Still holding my breath, I peer closely at the *"Privada"* file. It's just a short note in Spanish. It's signed "V."

So these are Veronica's files. Whoever Veronica is.

I feel very guilty doing this. But I also feel like a super spy, trying to get to the bottom of this ghost mystery.

I print out the entries for 10 *enero* and 12 *enero*. I try to translate them. My Spanish isn't that good yet, so I run inside and get Gran's big Spanish-English dictionary. I finally make some sense of what they say. In English it goes something like this:

```
January 10

Dear Father—

You are taking forever to die. Is it
because you cannot go until you apolo-
gize? Until you tell the truth?

I am waiting for your money. I am wait-
ing for you to finally confess. God
```

```
willing, it will be soon. I pray I only
have to be your dutiful daughter a few
more days.
```

```
                      v.
```

Daughter? Was Veronica the daughter of the man who died? The ghost guy?

Veronica does not sound even halfway nice. So she was waiting for her father's money? Was money more important than her father was? Why did she hate him so much?

I translate the second printout:

```
January 12

Father—
You do not eat today. A sign that you
will soon be dead. I wish that I had
friends to talk to here, but I do not.

You know why.
```

```
                      v.
```

Okay, that's enough. I fold the printouts in half and stuff them into my pocket. I really crossed a line here. Brrr! I have goose bumps.

But I can't help wondering... Did Veronica die too, right here in our Rapunzel *casita?* We know her father died here and that she hated him. Is it possible that...no...I don't want to think it, but...well, I do think it.

Is it possible that she...murdered...her own father?

I feel sick. I should not have been reading these. They're going to give me nightmares.

Still, I can't wait to tell someone. If our e-mail were hooked up, I'd fire off a note to Sam this very second. Then maybe her mom could translate everything for me and get it over with.

I can't get Gran all worked up over this. Okay, okay: I don't want her to know I invaded a dead person's privacy. And I won't see Lili until tomorrow evening—excuse me, eight in the afternoon. Darn!

After a little more tortilla soup, I take a walk with Gran. It's hard for me not to say anything about those secret files. But the walk does distract me a little.

We head down our cobblestone street, all musical now with tweeting birds. We pass terra-cotta and rose-colored houses with huge wooden doors.

"People used to drive their horse-drawn carriages straight through these doors in the sixteenth and seventeenth centuries," explains Gran.

No wonder they're so enormous! I think.

We end up at the *Jardín* in front of the pink church. Kids are rolling around in the gazebo, playing like puppies. Whole families are hanging out together—teens, grandparents, moms and dads—all laughing and snacking on treats: popcorn, fresh fruit cups, chile candy.

We get ice cream cones—pistachio for me, pomegranate ice for Gran—and I link my arm through hers the way I see other kids doing with their parents and grandparents. I would never be seen in public like this at home. But here we are, strolling arm in arm, past the balloon man and the tubby newspaper vendor, in the middle of Mexico.

Things are buzzing around us and I feel like I'm buzzing inside, too.

"I wish Mom could be here," I tell Gran. The happiness around here is contagious and it would do her good.

"She'll be here visiting before you know it," says Gran, winking. "You watch."

When I get home to bed, my whole happy feeling changes. It's dark, and there's an uneasiness in the air. Outside, banana fronds wave their long arms like ghosts in the moonlight. Leaves flicker in the breeze and brush up against the windows. I'm wishing I didn't know anything about Veronica, the greedy *fantasma*.

I make myself think about Mom instead. Maybe that treatment center will be good for her. Maybe the therapists there will help her get rid of her ghosts. That's probably what Gran was talking about when she said we all have ghosts. Things following us around, scaring us. Unfinished business.

It's weird, but it seems like Dad just drove off and left everything behind with no problem: me, Mom, and all his ghosts. Just left and never thought about any of us again. Not so far, at least. Mom's different. She cares a lot. So maybe her ghosts are harder to shoo away.

What am I doing, thinking about ghosts again? Now I'm back up, creeping across the room to get those printouts from my pocket. And the paperback Spanish dictionary I brought with me.

I hurry back to bed, pull the comforter up to my eyes, and clutch Farley to my chest. I unfold the sheets of paper and do my best translating again, in case I was wrong.

Unfortunately, I think I'm right.

I stare at Veronica's words in the moonlight. In Spanish, they're just a bunch of words to me. But when their meaning finally comes through in English, I'm chilled to the bone.

```
Taking forever to die. Money. Confess.
You know why.
```

Why did I go and read this stuff again? It's as if I can't help myself. Like I'm obsessed. Or...maybe this is how it feels to be possessed.

By a ghost.

# 8

# Starstruck

The next afternoon at seven P.M. sharp I cram into my snuggest jeans and a T-shirt. No long skirt. No frilly white top. Then I head straight next door to Lili's. I can't wait to tell her about Veronica.

Our street is decorated with bright plastic banners strung from one roof to the next. Red, white, and green—colors that say "Christmas" to me. But here I know they mean "Mexico." They're the colors of the national flag.

Dogs are pacing along the edges of the flat rooftops, wagging tongues and tails and being nosy about who I am and what I'm doing.

Four little kids are giggling on Lili's front stoop, getting tickled by Lili's dad. Señor Sanchez shakes my hand warmly and introduces me to Lili's sister and brothers: Isabel, Ricardo, César, and Paco.

"¡Hola!" I say. "¡Hola! ¡Hola! ¡Hola!" Gran had clued me in that it's better to greet everyone individually. If you don't say hi to each of them, sometimes their feelings get hurt. She must be right, because now the kids all jump up at once.

*"¡Venga, venga!"* they shout, pulling on my hands and leading me into the kitchen. "Come on!"

Inside the Sanchez *casa* it's all white plaster walls and plain wood furniture. I try not to look surprised when I see what's hanging on the kitchen wall: the Virgin Mary with red and green twinkle lights blinking around her frame. On. Off. On. Off.

"I have big news, Margarita!" Lili announces.

I nod, but I'm staring at Señora Sanchez. She's braiding Lili's hair and wrapping it into a figure eight shape with tiny pink flowers tucked in. Real flowers. It stops my heart from beating for a second. I wish my mom would do that sometime. Before I can say hola, Lili starts in.

*"¡Mira!* Look at this!" she says, waving a newspaper clipping in my face. As her mom finishes weaving in a few more blossoms, I read the announcement:

CASTING PARA ACTORES
Buscamos actores extras para una película.
8 P.M. martes y miércoles al hotel Elena.
Todas edades. Se filmará en agosto.
500 pesos por día.


CASTING CALL
We will be casting for movie extras roles at 8 P.M.
Tuesday and Wednesday at the Hotel Elena.
Filming will take place in August. All ages, all ethnicities.
500 pesos per day.

Wow. I forget all about my Veronica news for now. "Do you think they're casting kids?" I ask.

"Yes, all ages!" says Lili, pointing to the ad. "It's a real Hollywood movie. And see, the ad is in English, too, so they want many people!"

Señora Sanchez tells us in Spanish that she's heard they're filming before school starts.

"We can go down to the Hotel Elena and sign up tonight! What do you think?" asks Lili.

"Will we have to try out?" I ask. I've tried out for school plays before, when you read lines from a script. I'm actually a pretty good actress, if I do say so myself. And I like memorizing lines. But a movie? How do you try out for a real movie?

"Who knows?" says Lili, shrugging her shoulders. "But everybody is going. My friends, my mother, my brothers and sister. You must invite Abuelita Susi, too!"

"Gran would like that," I say. Can you imagine Gran and me in a movie? I can.

"If they pick us, it's *mucho dinero,* and...guess what else?" Now Lili is caught up in pure joy. She's jumping up and down and clapping her hands. "Guess who is the star of the film?"

I'm not exactly up on my Mexican movie stars.

"Alonzo Luna!" she blurts out.

Alonzo Luna? Well, I sure know *him.* He's a major Mexican American star. Twenty-six. Single. Sign: Scorpio. A total babe! My heart is pounding.

"Alonzo Luna?" I repeat.

"Plus five hundred pesos—fifty U.S. dollars a day!" adds Lili excitedly. "You want to do it?"

"Yes! *¡Sí, sí, sí!*" I shout, jumping up and down right along with Lili. Her brothers and sister grab me and give me a big group hug. I seem suddenly to be part of the family. They pull me toward the front door.

"Wait!" I say, giggling at the wild enthusiasm. "I can't go like this. Don't we want to look really, really good?"

"You do look good!" Isabel says in English. She reaches up and touches my hair.

"Curly," she says, smiling.

"Thanks," I tell her. I know I could look better, though. I wish I had flowers in my hair like Lili.

While the rest of the family goes to tell Gran the news, Lili and I head to the bathroom to raid her mother's makeup drawer. For the next twenty minutes we work on ourselves. We brush on blush, then line our lips with dark rose pencil, Mexican-style, and fill them in with pale pink frost. We make pouty mouths and model movie-star poses in the mirror.

When we're finished I touch Lili's shoulder with my thumb, making sizzle sounds. *"¡Estamos caliente, amiga!"* I say. It's true. We *do* look hot.

Lili's jaw drops in shock. "Margarita, you should *never* say that!" she tells me. "It's very rude!"

"Oh, I'm so sorry!" I say. I'm confused. Guess I've got a lot to learn about what I'm not supposed to be saying in Spanish. I switch to English.

"We look fabulous," I say, striking another pose.

Hollywood, here we come!

# 9
## Mucho Excitement

So here's what happens at a tryout for extras: After Señor Sanchez drives you in his taxi across town to a ritzy hotel, you go into a meeting room. The casting crew sits at a table up front, and whatever they're doing, there's a lot of jumping up, running around, and shouting going on.

You can't really see who's up there because you have to wait in line with about two hundred other people. Some of them look like experienced actors, which means very bored and snooty.

Our little group, eight of us including Gran, have ear-to-ear smiles. We don't mind waiting at all because maybe we have a chance be in movie with...keep your voice down...*Alonzo Luna!*

The hardest part for me and Lili is to keep each other from screaming out loud with excitement. Or leaping around like a couple of jumping beans or little kids who've just consumed large amounts of sugar. We wouldn't want to look unprofessional.

We quietly practice our throaty actress voices while we wait.

"Oh, Alonzo," Lili croons in a deep tone.

"What an honor it is to meet you," I say, but I can't get my voice as husky as Lili's.

About an hour later, when it's your turn at the table, you write down your name (i.e., Margarita Flynn) and your costume size, shoe size, and the color of your eyes. Gran helps when I come to the phone number.

Then you can also write notes. Lili helps me translate my note into Spanish. I put down "A very good screamer." I figure you can't hold back when you know you have a special gift, and opportunity is knocking.

After that, this too-cute guy from Mexico City with leather pants and spiky, shiny hair snaps your picture and tells you you're *muy bonita,* very beautiful. If you're a guy, he tells you you're *muy guapo,* very handsome.

That's it.

"That's it?" I ask Gran, appalled. There's no talking? Don't we have to read lines from a script? Don't I get to show off my scream?

"That's it," says Gran.

"Okay," I say, disappointed.

Then you go home and hope they call you.

The big rumor flying around the tryouts room is that the costumes are the very same ones they used in *Titanic,* and if it's true, I have to, *have to,* have to get a callback! Can't you see me with my hair all swept up and a few tendrils curling around my face, wearing a Kate Winslet dress that Leo DiCaprio had his arms around?

*Adiós,* Hayley! *Bienvenido, Margarita la Bonita!*

Of course, in the midst of all the tryout excitement, I slip my two secret computer notes to Lili.

"We have to talk later," I whisper. *"Fantasma* talk."

Lili's eyebrows shoot up with curiosity. But every time we try to discuss the ghost news, we get interrupted.

Now I'm home again with Gran, wondering if Lili's in bed yet.

Gran lights every candle in our front room nooks and crannies and the little saints glow. They look very holy with their golden halos and their eyes gazing up to heaven. Gran settles into her favorite comfy chair and tucks a serape blanket around her legs. She wants to rehash all the details of the tryouts.

"I bring my granddaughter to Mexico and she ends up in Hollywood!" she teases. She's getting a kick out of all this.

"How about you, Gran?" I say. "This may be the start of your new career."

Gran chuckles. "Your grandfather used to tell me I looked just like Audrey Hepburn, the movie star. My, my, love is blind, isn't it? If he could see me now..." She laughs. It makes me happy to know Gran's happy, too.

In the flickering candlelight, the rock walls look like a haunted medieval castle, which makes me feel slightly spooked. Maybe my grandfather *can* see Gran now. Maybe he's a ghost, too. This place is definitely made for ghosts.

My mind starts revving up again. Veronica lived here, sat within these rocks, probably lit candles at night. Did she murder her father in this very room? I wonder. Then I think, What if she's the jealous type? What if she's jealous that I'm probably going to be a movie star soon?

"Do you mind if I go visit Lili for a few minutes?" I ask. I'm thinking of dragging Lili back to the chicken coop for some computer time. Is this me talking, or that nasty little red devil?

"That's fine, honey," says Gran. "But don't stay too late. We've all had a busy day." She's already snuggled up with a book.

I'm feeling jittery as I walk out to the garden with the flashlight. All the turquoise eyes are staring at me from the tin tree masks and the moon is making long, trembly shadows everywhere.

I knock on Lili's door and when she answers, I ask her to come over. She quietly talks to her mom and then slips out to join me.

"I have only twenty minutes," she whispers. "I have to put the *chicos* to bed soon."

I see the printouts clutched in her hand. *¡Excelente!* The door of my chicken sanctuary creaks as we open it. I pull up the files.

"See? They're from January until March," I say.

"That's exactly when the *señora* came to live with the old man," says Lili, nodding. "So now we know the woman's name was Veronica."

"And she was his daughter," I add.

"We have time to read one more tonight," Lili whispers.
Click.
Open.
Lili translates.

```
February 5

Our neighbors are shooting off fireworks
again, Father. Do you hear them? They
```

seem happy. Would they be so happy if
they knew who you really are?

Maybe the money will help to make up for
your sins.

v.

"Sins?" I ask. "Who *was* that guy? What does she
mean?"

"I have no idea," says Lili. "But something is very dark
here."

I agree. This Veronica woman is just plain ugly. Not a
compassionate bone in her body. Her father was dying, for
heaven's sake! And how bad could he have been that she
couldn't forgive him? That all she wanted was his money?

I may not be happy with my own dad at the moment,
but compared with Veronica, well...

We shut down the computer.

"I wonder how Veronica died," I say.

"Do we really want to know?" Lili asks.

Maybe not. "It sounds like some terrible secret between
them was kept hidden," I say, shuddering.

It's already time for Lili to go. We give each other
frightened looks. Who knows where Veronica's ghost may
be hiding? In this jungle garden? Out by the door? On the
street in front of Lili's house?

"Do you want me to walk you home?" I ask, secretly
hoping Lili will say no.

Lili shakes her head. "Then you will have to walk back
home alone," she says. Both of us stand outside the sanctuary, not moving.

"Well, I'll walk you halfway to your front door," I suggest. "Then I'll be halfway from my front door. Then we'll both run inside at the same time."

"Good idea," Lili says.

When Lili and I separate, I race on tiptoe through the street door, back across the garden, and into our candlelit house. I kiss Gran goodnight, scramble up the spiral staircase, and hop in bed with Farley.

Boom! The minute I settle in fireworks start bursting and a shower of glittery pink and emerald hits the skylights over my head, like I'm in the middle of a cascade of sparkly stars. Beautiful!

All the church bells are ringing at once. Gran rushes upstairs for a look-see.

"*Gracias,* Father Hidalgo," she cries. "Because of you, we get fireworks!"

"Who's Father Hidalgo?" I ask.

"He was the Father of Mexican Independence!" she says grandly. "Today is the anniversary of his death."

"Is that why our street had red, white, and green flags hanging everywhere?" I ask.

"Not just our street, sweetie," Gran says. "All the streets!"

I must have been so thrilled about the tryouts, I didn't even notice.

Gran is like a little girl sitting on my bed and getting all excited every time a new twinkling firework-blossom explodes.

For some reason I think of Veronica. Did she sit here? Did she lie on this bed, watching fireworks burst overhead? I wonder. Did she *die* in this bed?

I need to shake this creepy stuff out of my head. "Tell me the story of Father Hidalgo, Gran," I say.

"Oh, he was a very courageous man," says Gran, switching to her storytelling voice, which is very soothing.

Good. I can tell this will be a long story. It will put me to sleep.

"In 1810, Father Hidalgo, a priest, stood in front of his parish church just a few miles from here. He ripped down the Spanish flag and held up a banner of the Virgin of Guadalupe. At that moment it became the flag of Mexican Independence. He started a revolution."

"I'm surprised the Spanish soldiers didn't shoot him," I say. I'm picturing the crowd of Mexicans supporting Father Hidalgo, shouting the way the townspeople are right now as they watch the fireworks.

"Oh, they did shoot him," says Gran. "In a firing squad. Then they chopped off his head and stuck it on a pole to scare the Mexican people from trying to fight for their independence anymore."

Gulp. Not exactly the bedtime story I had in mind.

"Did that stop the Mexican people?" I ask.

"Of course not," says Gran. "This was their country. They didn't want to live in New Spain, which is what the Spanish named it. They struggled on, fighting..."

I like stories of people struggling on, fighting for what they know is right and fair. I hug Farley and burrow in deeper. I listen to Gran's storytelling voice and watch the little sparkles of fireworks as they ping-ping me to sleep.

# 10
# The Princess Goes to School

Pow! Bang! Fireworks are exploding again, waking me up. Are they *still* partying? I sit up to check out the scene from my observatory.

I don't see any fireworks in the sky. No more dancing in the streets. The sun is shining, and those roosters and ducks and pigs next door are crowing and quacking and snorting. I glance at my clock. Seven A.M. Early. But it's too noisy to sleep, so I get up.

When I go downstairs for breakfast, a giant polka-dot rooster is standing under the spiral stairs, staring up at me. Paintbrush in hand, Gran is touching up his purple eyes.

"Meet Pablo," she announces. Pablo is made of papier-mâché and is ruby red with yellow spots. "I just moved him from my library. He makes a nice pet, doesn't he?"

"Lovely. And we don't even need to feed him," I point out. "Or take him for walks."

"Exactly," Gran agrees, chuckling.

"So what's with the fireworks?" I ask.

"Oh, they're just rockets. Firecrackers, actually, called *cohetes*," Gran says, wiping her brush on a towel.

"Everyone is still celebrating Father Hildalgo. They'll be shooting them off for a few more days. Starting at five."

"Five in the *morning?*" I repeat. I knew I hadn't been sleeping that well the last few hours. I was having nightmares of firing squads and bloody heads. Not to mention noisy resident ghosts. No wonder.

"They say that early in the morning when it's quiet in town, God can hear them," says Gran, as if setting off firecrackers at daybreak is the most natural thing in the world. "Now, come have some breakfast."

As I digest my cornflakes, I'm also digesting the idea that people think God is listening for fireworks. At five o'clock in the morning.

"So what's up for today, Gran?" I ask.

"It's the Feast of St. Ignatius. I thought we'd celebrate by checking out your new school," she says, cutting mango slices.

"Saint *who?*" I ask.

"Ignatius Loyola. He was born in Spain," she explains, setting out the mango for me. I've noticed that you can ask Gran anything and she always has details to spout off. "He founded the Jesuit order of priests. They still teach hundreds of thousands of students every year. The best educators on planet Earth."

"Can you tell me more about this new school?" I ask.

Gran chuckles. "Don't worry, *tesoro.* I think you'll really like this school. It'll be a nice surprise."

A big gulp of cornflakes gets stuck in my throat. We'll see, I think.

Twenty minutes later we're heading down the cobblestone streets toward my new educational institution. I've put on a flowered skirt and a long-sleeved T-shirt for the occasion. Formal is better, I figure, if there are going to be priests and nuns and pictures of saints in the classrooms.

People everywhere are lugging stuff to and from the market: huge paintings, bouquets of flowers, tinkling chandeliers, bags of flour and rice. Giant cheese puff pillows. You can barely fit a car down these narrow streets, so the people are pros at using their heads or their backs or their shoulders to carry things around. They don't seem to mind. Most of them have big smiles on their faces.

Gran stops in front of an ancient castle. Over the arched entrance is a sign in gold letters: *"La Escuela de Artes."* The School of Arts.

"My new school?" I ask, amazed. "My school is a *castle?*" With all these fairy-tale settings, I'm going to start thinking I'm a real princess.

"It's an old convent," Gran explains, ringing the bell. A very cute boy with spiky gelled-up hair lets us in. He introduces himself as Bronco. I give him my brightest smile and he smiles back.

We enter a courtyard bordered by arched walkways like the ones I saw once in a movie about monks. In the middle is a fountain surrounded by flowers and white café tables and chairs.

"Señora Susana. Señorita Margarita," says a crisp woman Bronco brought us to meet. I shoot a grateful look at Gran. She's told them my name is Margarita. The woman is the headmistress. Her white blouse and blue suit are very well ironed, and she's wearing high heels that click-click-click on the stone floors.

"I am Señora Gomez, and I welcome you," she says, shaking hands. She leads us up a wide marble staircase with gigantic murals painted on the walls. My eyes must be as big as tortillas as I stare at the art—paintings of workers who are farming or building or lugging heavy stuff around. I can't say they look joyful like the people we passed on the streets. They're just working hard.

"One of Rivera's students painted that mural in the 1940s," notes Señora Gomez. She's talking about Diego Rivera, the famous painter we studied in Ms. Stucky's class, the one married to another painter, Frida Kahlo.

"Rivera, of course, was born here in our state of Guanajuato," says the headmistress. "And this entire room was done by David Siqueiros, another great Mexican muralist." I'm completely quiet. Stunned. This is like being in church for some people. I'm surrounded by the original work of some of the finest artists who ever lived. Talk about inspiration!

Gran smiles, happy that I like the surprise she planned for me.

"It's amazing, isn't it, *tesoro?*" she whispers. I can only nod.

"All the classes are in English, but taught by Spanish-speaking teachers," says Señora Gomez, showing us the classrooms.

"Except Spanish classes, of course!" I quip, trying to keep things light.

*"Excepto las clases de español, por supuesto,"* she repeats seriously.

Every classroom door Señora Gomez opens is carved with calla lilies or suns or moons.

The library has shelves stacked to the ceiling with gleaming wood ladders to help you get to the out-of-reach books. The Spanish classroom has verbs conjugated in frames on the walls, mixed with fantastic art of dancing skeletons and flowery skulls. Even the math room has a display of art. Above the fractions still scribbled on the board from last semester hang devil masks that could scare the pants off you.

My mouth drops open when we look at the art room. I see hundreds of brushes in tin cans lined up along the windowsills. Huge tables and easels splattered with years of paint. Colorful paint blotches all over the floor. I wonder if Diego or Frida left their paint speckles here.

I don't want to leave this room. I'm itching to pick up a brush and paint something. But Señora Gomez is efficiently herding us down to the outdoor café by the entry fountain. She orders a trio of *mocha machos*—icy drinks made from chocolate and coffee laced with cinnamon.

I try to tear my eyes away from the golden-green hummingbird on the lily beside me as we discuss my classes. I'm taking painting and Spanish, of course. And math and Mexican history and geography. I get to choose one other subject, an elective. I can't decide. Maybe mask-making. Maybe indigenous dance.

"There are quite a few other *gringos* you'll meet who study here as well, Margarita," says the headmistress. *Gringo* is considered a friendly word here. Actually, the right word is *gringa* if you're a *muchacha,* a girl, like me. But don't say *gringa* in Kalamazoo—it's kind of demeaning north of the border.

"See you in two weeks," says Señora Gomez as she

waves good-bye, shutting the huge front door behind us.

Gran and I go from store to store to get my supplies. It's not like there's a Target or Wal-Mart in town, so we buy notebooks and pens of every color in the *papelería,* the paper shop. We buy computer supplies in the computer shop. Then we go to TelMex and Gran buys a pink cell phone for me and a green one for her. She wants to be sure we're in touch all the time. I want to be sure Jorge can be in touch, so I'll need to give him this number.

"You'll have to show me how to use this little contraption," says Gran, looking at her cell like it's an alien being.

When we get home the phone is ringing and I scramble up the steps to get it, hoping it's the casting director.

I answer with a Mexican-style hello. *"¿Bueno?"* I say in my best throaty actress voice.

It's Mom. She's settled into her temporary home. She says it's comfortable and full of trees and the staff is nice. I can tell she's feeling nervous. So I tell her about that first night at Gran's and how weird I felt with the spooky masks and Cynthia the skeleton.

"It didn't last long, the weirdness," I say. "Now I really like it here, and Gran's the best!"

"Oh good," she says, sounding relieved. But I can tell she's still got that emptiness inside her. Why does it transfer right through the phone and make me feel empty, too?

"Don't feel guilty, Mom," I reassure her. "I like Mexico even more than I thought I would. It's awesome. And I bet you'll like it there, too. They'll take good care of you."

I hope.

I tell her about Lili and my school and the tryouts.

"You tried out for a movie?" she asks.

"Yeah, Mom. A made-for-TV movie that you'll be able to watch in Kalamazoo!" I tell her.

"Wow! That's wonderful, sweetie," she says. She's perking up. Maybe now my happiness is contagious, traveling through the phone to her.

I give her my new cell phone number.

"Call me whenever you want," I tell her.

"You, too, honey," she says. I tell her how much I miss her, which I do.

When I hang up, I'm feeling a bit glum. I'm praying Mom's depression will get fixed and she'll be happy like I remember her being when I was little. I go down to the kitchen where Gran is squishing avocados out of their skins for guacamole.

"How's your mom?" asks Gran.

"Pretty good, I think...What do you think she does at that place, Gran?" I ask.

She sets the guac and chips on the table and ruffles my hair gently.

"Your mom has been put on medication. And she's meeting with therapists every day to get to the bottom of what's making her so sad."

Well, that's a no-brainer. I could have told them why she's sad.

"It's all because my stupid dad left," I say, cracking a chip to bits in my hand. I don't even realize how mad I am until I see what my hand did.

"Remember, *tesoro,* she was sad for quite a spell before your dad left. So it's probably something more than that.

His leaving was just the straw that broke the camel's back, as they say."

I don't want to think it's more than Dad leaving us. Does that mean Mom might be crazy or something?

"What made her sad all that time before Dad left?" I ask, almost afraid to hear the answer. Did it have something to do with *me?* Some secret I don't know about?

"Well, it has nothing to do with you," Gran reassures me, as if she has read my mind. "Some of it has to do with how your mom lets your dad run her life. How your mom lost her own self along the way."

"I wish I could fix everything," I whisper. I feel that vinegary feeling running through my bloodstream, like just before tears start. "I wish I could make her happy."

Gran puts her hand over mine. "That's not your job, Hayley," she tells me. "You can make yourself happy. *That's* your job."

We just sit here for a minute. I fiddle with the corn chip dust in my palm.

"You do your job and your mom will do hers," says Gran. "Okay?" She stands up and kisses me on the top of my head. "Now, why don't you go pop in on Lili? Ask her about where she's going to school this year."

Hmmm. What does that mean? I look up at Gran, and she's smiling a secret smile. I feel a little happy spark in my heart.

"Is she going to Bellas Artes, too?" I just about scream.

"Well, go ask her," says Gran, humming to herself as she clears our chips and guac.

"She *is* going to my school, isn't she?" I jump up and

race out through the garden. I open the street door. Whoa! Lili is standing on my stoop, ready to ring the bell. I just about blurt out the question about school when I stop myself. Lili's eyes are filled with tears.

"*¿Qué pasa?* What's wrong?" I ask.

"My papa," she whispers. "My papa is leaving."

# 11
# Parakeet Street

Oh no! Lili's dad is leaving? Just like *my* dad? I'm instantly furious. What's wrong with these idiot fathers? How can they just walk away and turn their backs on wonderful kids like Lili? Like me?

I grab Lili's hand and lead her to the blue bench in our garden. We sit down.

"Tell me," I say.

"My d-dad has to..." Lili stutters, sniffling into her Kleenex. "He has to...go up to the U.S. again."

What, does he have a girlfriend there or something? I think. But I don't say it. I'm raging mad.

"Why?" I ask.

"To make some money," says Lili.

"Oh," I say. I feel terrible about what I'd been thinking. Maybe this isn't anything like my dad and his leaving me and Mom.

"Is he coming back?" I ask cautiously.

Lili looks me square in the face, her eyes shocked. "Of course he's coming back, Margarita! But he'll be gone for three, maybe four months."

Inside I'm feeling just a little jealous. Three or four months doesn't sound bad at all to me. I mean, Señor Sanchez loves his family. He's going to come back to them. With my dad, who knows? Lili is actually lucky, compared to me. I guess it's true what they say about how misery loves company. But I try not to compare our separate Dad sorrows while I listen.

It turns out that the five hundred pesos Lili will make on days when she works in the film is practically the same amount of money her dad earns here in an entire week. Only fifty dollars! He drives a cab when he's here in San Miguel, and he sells birds, too.

He has a sign on his cab that says *"Taxi y Pajaritos."* Taxi and Birds. He sells canaries and parakeets and cockatiels. Every Tuesday he balances their cages on his head like a stack of tweeting hats. Then he walks up the street to where his taxi is parked. He fills his cab with bamboo birdcages and drives to the market.

I'd never seen parakeet or canary eggs until I came to San Miguel. Señor Sanchez's birds make nests and lay eggs all the time, and then the squeaky babies stick their heads out. They're adorable. You can hear his birds chirping all the way to the end of the block, so Gran and I call our street Parakeet Street.

"When is he leaving?" I ask.

"He goes in five days."

"And what kind of work will he do?"

"He and my uncles are going to pick fruit. They make a lot of money," Lili tells me. "It just makes me sad that he has to go there and be away from us."

"Can't he make money here doing something different?"

I ask, putting my arm around her shoulder. Then I think of how he already has *two* jobs. Plus Lili's mom is a housekeeper for some of the neighbors, including Gran. That's three jobs, and the Sanchez family is still what you'd call poor in Kalamazoo.

"There is no money in Mexico," Lili says sadly.

I guess it's true. The tourists have money. Gran has her Social Security check, which doesn't go very far in the U.S., but here it's three times what Señor Sanchez earns. Very few people around here can afford new cars or computers or vacations.

"This time he's going to Michigan," Lili says. "To pick grapes. And maybe pumpkins in October."

"Near Kalamazoo?" I ask.

"I don't know exactly," says Lili.

Señor Sanchez is going to be one of those Michigan migrant workers I don't know one thing about! They just seem to stay quietly in their trailers when they're not working in the fields. It makes me sad to think what I've heard other people say about them.

They're uneducated. They can't even speak English.

They're so sneaky, coming across the border like they do.

They're taking jobs from Americans.

Of course I don't tell Lili this stuff, because that's the last thing she needs to hear. She's sad enough that her dad has to leave his family for three months.

*"Vamos a ver,"* says Lili, which is what she always says when it's time to change the subject. "We'll see what happens." She wipes her eyes and sits up straight.

"You want to hang out for a while?" I ask.

"Sure. Hang out," says Lili, smiling a little. "It's a funny expression, hang out."

"It is," I agree. Then I lower my voice. "We could check out more notes from our ghost."

"I've been thinking, maybe it's not a good idea to be reading those," Lili says slowly. "It's bad energy, Margarita. We might be inviting *la fantasma* back—How do you say it?—in a big way."

"Maybe you're right," I say. But the little red devil is whispering in my ear even as I reply. We sit through another long silence. Then Lili's eyes meet mine and they have a devious spark in them.

"To tell you the truth, I'm still curious," she admits.

I perk up. "So you want to translate?"

"Okay," she says.

A pig lets out a squeal next door.

"Did you know that woman over there has a whole farm in her backyard?" I ask Lili as we head to my chicken sanctuary.

"Yes. She loves animals," says Lili. "But I've heard she hates people."

"Really?"

*"De veras,"* she says. "She is very strange. Everyone calls her *la Bruja.*"

"The witch? Hmmm... What's her real name?" I ask.

"We don't even know. Isn't that terrible? All the neighbors know each other, but not her. If you say hello, she pretends like she does not hear you."

"Is she an old lady?" I ask. I can't tell from my window, since she's always covered in scarves and shawls and men's clothes.

"I do not know that, either. She has lived there for a few years and we know nothing about her. We think she never leaves her house."

"But she has to go shopping sometimes, doesn't she?" I ask.

"Maybe she has everything she needs from her garden and her animals," says Lili. "It's a mystery."

I'd say there's a lot of mystery going on in this town. Once I bring up the files, I scoot over to give Lili my chair. She reads the next letter silently, her brows knitted together.


```
February 1


Father,
Just die and give me my freedom.
```

V

"Veronica was like *la Bruja,* I suppose. So alone," says Lili. "We never really saw what she looked like. All I know is that she was only here for, oh…maybe two or three months. Then her father died."

"Do you think… Could *he* be the ghost? Or did she die here and she is the ghost?" I ask. I have shivers now.

*"No sé,"* says Lili. "I don't know." I see her shudder, too. "The man's body was brought out one night and we all gathered in the street. The police said the ambulance came too late, that he was dead already."

"Lili," I whisper, "what if she murdered him?"

Lili stared at me. "Murdered her father?"

"Where was Veronica that night?" I ask. "She had to be here to call the ambulance. Then where did she go?"

"Some people said she was already in the ambulance with him by the time we got out on the street. Some people said she was still in the house."

"And then?"

"People came with food and flowers for her, but she never answered the door. The gifts piled up on the front stoop. That's when rumors started that maybe she was dead, too. That the house was haunted."

"So we don't know if Veronica is dead or alive. And we don't know how her father really died," I point out.

"Well, the police said he died from natural causes."

"So there was no reason to investigate," I say.

"No. But I don't think they tried very hard to discover the cause of death. He was old. He was sick. Why should the police care how he died? We never heard anything again."

"Not until that girl Angela moved in, right?"

"That's right," says Lili, nodding. "And the next thing that happened was that Señora Susi bought the house a year later."

Who did Gran buy the house from? I wonder. I have to find out.

We hear Lili's mom calling for her. She jumps up.

"I have to go," she says. "Why don't you print out the other notes? Then I'll translate them when I can."

"Deal!" I say as Lili rushes off.

While the printer is cranking out the files, I get busy on an important project. I line up my paint tubes in the chicken boxes—reds in one, greens in another, yellows, oranges, blues, purples—until it looks like a rainbow in here.

Then I take an old scrap of wood and start painting my sign for over the door, in red with metallic gold outlines:

MARGARITA'S SANCTUARY
(No *Fantasmas* Allowed!)

# 12
# Scorpions and Red Hair

I take my sketchbook to bed and draw pages and pages of my No *Fantasmas* Allowed sign. I do the lettering in a flowery style, then Gothic, then in Spanish, then in English. For some dumb reason, it makes me feel safe. Until the middle of the night, that is, when I'm fast asleep and something hits me in the face. Something light and creepy.

I bolt straight up in bed just in time to see a really nasty-looking creature skitter down my arm and under my pillow.

"Scorpion!" I scream. "A scorpion jumped on my face!"

I leap out of bed and race around in circles, shaking out my hair and shrieking that I have to go back to Kalamazoo right this very minute. I've never seen a scorpion before in my life. But when you see one, believe me, you know *exactly* what it is.

"I cannot live with prehistoric Mexican bugs falling from the rafters!" I holler as Gran comes rushing up to save me. "Poisonous, evil, disgusting bugs!"

I'm still shaking. When I get that wound up, I can't stop.

"It's just a teeny brown one, and it's hardly poisonous,"

Gran says calmly, taking a look-see. She whacks it with a shoe.

"Those things can sting you to death with their nasty tails, can't they?" I squeal. I'm trembling, all shook up.

"No, sweetie, they can't," says Gran. "Not the kind of scorpions we get here. They're pretty harmless, unless you're very allergic."

Still. I'm lucky I didn't get stung on the nose. Or *up* the nose, inside my nostril. Or in the eyes, or way inside my ear...Oh gross!

"Did you know these critters eat each other alive sometimes?" Gran asks, picking up the scorpion's dead body with a tissue.

"That's a little too much information for me," I say, shuddering.

Gran and I both head for the bathroom. She's going to flush the little carcass with its pointy pinchers down the toilet. Me, I'm going to take a shower and wash my hair extra well in case there's a stray leg left in there someplace.

I start wondering how that thing got there. Is it possible the ghost dropped that scorpion right on me? Is it possible the dead man was very allergic to scorpions and that's how Veronica killed him?

Is-it-possible thoughts keep me up until dawn, when I tear off my sheets and pillowcases. I bring them downstairs to be washed by Lili's mom, who comes in once a week to keep house for us. At first it seemed weird to me that Señora Sanchez works for Gran, but Gran says it is a good way for her to make extra money for the family.

Gran's already awake and has set up her sewing machine at the kitchen table. She says her project for the day is to sew insect netting for around my bed. A nice protective canopy to keep any creepy critters out.

"That's only the third scorpion I've ever seen in this house," says Gran as she stitches a seam. "Say," she suggests, "why don't you give Lili a holler?" To make up for my nasty night, she wants to treat me and Lili to a little spa time. She'll make us an appointment at La Chiquita Salon. We can get manicures and whatever else we want.

"A back-to-school treat," she says.

"That's so nice, Gran!" I give her a hug and grab my phone. I've never had a manicure except when Sam and I have done our nails together, but that's different. This will be at a real spa.

I'm surprised to find out that Lili and her friends have been to La Chiquita before. It turns out that Lupe, the owner, is Lili's mother's cousin.

"It's great there. But you never know how you'll look when you leave," Lili warns me. It all depends on Lupe's mood and what products she has in stock at the moment.

"I'm up for an adventure," I tell Lili.

"Me, too," she says.

I'm thinking I don't just want a manicure. I want to have my hair tinted for the first time, to spice up the squirrelly look. I casually drop a hint to Gran, reminding her that I'm almost thirteen, an actual teenager.

"*¿Cómo no?* Why not? You do what will make you feel good for your first day of school," she says.

Wow! I dash out the door before she comes to her senses and changes her mind.

"Just don't come back turquoise," she calls from her sewing corner.

"I promise!" I holler back, taking a quick detour to pick up the Veronica printouts hidden in my sanctuary.

Lili and I walk across town and over a stone bridge to the shops along the creek. We come to a dinky place with a sign that says *"Casa de Belleza y Spa"* in bright purple letters. Beauty Parlor and Spa. It's not quite the soothing atmosphere I was expecting.

Lupe only has one chair, and outside in back are chaise lounges you lie on to read magazines while you wait. Lupe's laundry hangs on the line to the right, and there's a massage table to the left. She has a garden hose hooked up through the back door for washing and rinsing our hair, and she has six boxes of hair color and two bottles of nail polish on her shelf.

"Coca-Cola?" Lupe asks. She hands us each a cool can and a straw.

Lili and I take turns. Whoever's not getting beautified is out lying on a lounge, reading the secret files. We discover nothing new. All the same mysterious references to sins and money and dying. We'll have to expand our detective work if we want to discover the true story of *la fantasma.*

When it's my beauty time I ask Lupe for a hair tint just a shade brighter than what I have now. Lili asks for pale pink nails and just a trim on her hair. She ends up with a short, spunky little ponytail. We both come out with Geranium Red nails.

When Gran sees my hair that afternoon she nearly drops her garden spade. It's red. No, it's orange. Orange like a mango. Orange like a Halloween pumpkin. It's a bit harsh against my pale skin. Okay, very harsh.

"So is this the Hollywood version of you?" Gran asks. She has a wheelbarrow full of flowers she's in the middle of planting. They're the kind that attracts butterflies, and the colors make your eyes jump: scarlet, fuchsia, sapphire, sun yellow.

I know my new hair is bright, but so is everything and everybody around me. Believe it or not, I think I'll fit in better here with mango orange hair than I did with squirrel fur. I hope I'm right. Besides, I have faith that after a few shampoos it will tone down.

"Say, Gran," I ask, slyly changing the subject. "Who sold you this house?"

"One of the real estate people in town," she answers. "I'm not sure I recall her name. She might have moved back to New York."

Darn! This is not helpful. But I decide to persist.

"So who was the previous owner? Did this house belong to one Mexican family for generations?" I'm trying to sound historically savvy.

"I don't have any idea, Hayley Cakes. My lawyer and their lawyer handled everything. I just knew it was a good deal, and I loved the place." Gran looks up, wiping her forehead with the back of her gardening glove. "Why?"

"Oh, nothing. Just curious, I guess."

Thankfully I'm saved by the front doorbell. Somebody is ringing, ringing, ringing.

"Did you get the call?" Lili yells through the little porthole on the street door before I even get there. "Did you get the call?"

# 13
## Señorita Hollywood

Jorge, the casting director for the movie, just called Lili back to be in the film. Her mom got called, too. "They didn't call me," I say, trying not to be too jealous. "Maybe I'm too *gringa*-looking or something."

"I am sure that is not the reason. They did not ask for *los chicos*, either," Lili says. She's talking about her little brothers and sisters.

I'm happy for Lili and her mom. But I'm disappointed for me. Just as Lili is giving me a genuinely sympathetic hug, Gran walks out with her green cell phone.

"It's for you, Señorita Hollywood," she whispers. "Good thing we gave them our new number."

Jorge? I grab the phone.

"*Sí...Sí...¡Sí!*" I answer to every one of Jorge's questions. "*¿Ahora? ¡Claro que sí!* Of course!" We movie stars have to leave now, *ahora,* immediately, and take a taxi to a warehouse just outside of town. I hang up and give big bear hugs to Gran and Lili.

"To get fitted for our costumes," I explain to Gran as I pretend to button up tiny silk buttons on the cuffs of my gloves, which I remember Kate Winslet doing in *Titanic*.

"I know," says Gran. "Yours truly is getting fitted, too."

"What? You got called too, Gran?" I ask.

"Yup. Jorge says I'm in."

"Yes!" I scream. This is great! *¡Fantástico!*

We stop by for Señora Sanchez. She's already called Lili's dad to pick us up.

"In his limousine," she teases. The *chicos* and their baby-sitter are jumping up and down, very excited that we got picked.

"I'm sorry they didn't call you guys," I tell them. "Next time, no?"

"Next time," says Isabel, who is definitely looking a bit sad to miss her chance at stardom. I make a note in my head to bring her back a movie souvenir of some kind.

Off we go in Señor Sanchez's taxi. Lili and I start waving the Queen Elizabeth wave to everybody we pass. We have to get the silliness out of our systems before we get to Wardrobe, where we want to act like coolheaded pros.

The warehouse is an old *hacienda,* all brick and stone and archways, another fairy-tale building. When we go inside, it's chaos. There are racks of clothes lined up like at Wal-Mart and a roomful of seamstresses sewing and ironing costumes. Too bad Gran didn't haul my bed netting along—these ladies would have me scorpion-proof in a jiffy.

People from Los Angeles and D.F. (which is short for Mexico City—they call it *Distrito Federal* in Spanish) are rushing around giving orders on cell phones in English and Spanish while they size you up with a tape measure. In a slightly uppity tone, they say things like this:

"That's not my job, darling."

"I'm up to my fanny in fittings here."

"Don't get your knickers in a knot, dear. Just send me a dozen hats. Pronto."

When they holler your name you go into one of the big dressing rooms with two women, hats, coats, boots, dresses, gloves, and a three-way mirror. You stand there in your underwear with your arms spread like wings while they put clothes and hats on you, tuck and pin and stand back and frown, and undress you and dress you again.

This must be exactly how princesses get dressed every day, I figure.

Finally they find just the right combination. Then they all smile and tell you how *bonita* and *guapa* and *hermosa* you look. Translation: Beautiful!

They're right. I look awesome. I hardly recognize my redheaded self in a white blouse with billowy sleeves and a lace collar pinned with a cameo. My skirt is tan with fancy black embroidered birds on it. My high-heeled boots are fastened with little pearl buttons. A wide-brimmed black velvet hat hides all but a few choice wisps of my orange curls. Luckily no one seems to notice that my hair color isn't what I said on my application.

"How much do you love this?" I ask Lili when she comes out looking gorgeous in a dark green silk dress with long gloves. Her hat has white flowers and a frothy ribbon of veil tied in a bow at the back. A white petticoat peeks out from the hem of her dress.

"*¡Muchissimo!*" she says. She's just radiant. We're both

going to be townspeople strolling down city streets. We don't know much more about the movie. The dressers have no idea what city the story is set in, or what day we'll film, or exactly what our roles are.

Next we have to get checked by the costume director, who's decked out in a tapestry vest and tapestry pants that give him a dining-room-drapes look. He slides his red sunglasses down on his nose, inspects our outfits, and gives us the thumbs up.

Then we put our shoes and gloves and hats and jewelry in plastic bags, which the wardrobe ladies attach to our costumes. Everything is tagged with our names and the scene we'll be in. Lili and I are in the same scene, which is called "1914 Winter Street."

"When will we be filming?" Lili asks the costume director on the way out.

"Soon. This week. Next week. In a few days. Not sure. Jorge will call you the day before the shoot," he tells us, waving us out with a flick of his cell phone.

"Okay, then," I say. They better not call us to shoot on a school day.

Gran and Señora Sanchez are still sitting on folding chairs, waiting to be called for their fittings. They're caught up in the hubbub like it's the best entertainment they've seen in years.

"Lili and I will be right outside, on the benches," I tell Gran.

As we leave we see our costumes hanging on either side of a military uniform on the rack labeled "1914 Winter Street." Our name tags are on them. "M. Flynn" and "L. Sanchez," they say.

The uniform in the middle is labeled "A. Luna."

Lili and I both have to shove our fists in our mouths so we won't scream until we're well outside the warehouse door, where nobody but the jackrabbits and stray dogs can hear us.

# 14

# My Parasite Fiesta

Did you ever plan a party for a whole neighborhood in *one* day? For like, two hundred people? I sure haven't, but that's exactly what me and Gran and the Sanchezs are doing. Yesterday, on our way home from the wardrobe fittings, we all decided to throw a Farewell Fiesta for Lili's dad. And when's the party? Today!

Luckily, we've been getting a lot of help. Since noon neighbors have been showing up loaded with stuff. There are balloons to blow up. A *piñata* to hang from a tree. Pink and green and orange and turquoise paper lanterns to attach to strings of lights. People are swarming all over Lili's backyard, busy as ants.

Me, I'm up on a wobbly wooden ladder. Lili and Isabel are handing me streamers that will stretch across the garden like a pink ceiling. The *chicos* are hanging a *"¡Te Amamos, Papá!"* banner over the front door to remind their dad how much they love him. Señora Sanchez and Gran are in the kitchen cooking up a storm.

By three o'clock Gran and I have finished our work and we go change into our party clothes. She puts on a long gathered skirt and an embroidered shawl. I decide on something too fancy for Kalamazoo, but perfect for here: my off-the-shoulder lacy white blouse over my jeans and big silver hoop earrings.

When we get back the Sanchez place is already one wild fiesta. Aunts and uncles, grandmas and grandpas have arrived. Busy *tías* and hungry *tíos* spread checkered cloths on food tables. Chubby *abuelas* stir pots over the grill. *Abuelos* tell jokes that I don't know enough Spanish to get. But I laugh anyway.

By evening I'm counting about forty-five kids and sixty relatives and a hundred neighbors. Everyone's brought a platter of food to add to the table, so there's a whole world of dishes for me to try.

Even though it's a going-away party, it's not one bit sad. Party lanterns glow as kids scramble for *piñata* candy. Some older boys are setting up humongous speakers, and then the music starts.

"Salsa!" shouts Lili. She dances with her dad. Señora Sanchez dances with the *chicos*. Of course Gran is out there doing a little salsa, too, her skirt whirling. Shoulders are waving, girls and grandmas are twirling. One of the uncles, Tío Paco, takes my hand and dances me around. I have no idea what I'm doing, but who cares? Nobody's judging. Everybody's just having a great time.

The whole time I'm salsa-ing I've got my eye on those tables, itching to get a taste of that food. Gran's warned me that there are more invisible parasites in Mexico than freckles on my whole body. Mexican people grow up with them, so they're immune. But we *gringos* can't drink water from the faucet or eat certain foods—Gran's told me all about them—because they have parasites that will stay in our systems and make us sick.

I'm not sure exactly what they look like, but I picture those ghostly amoebae and paramecia on the microscope slides they blow up at school. Do I want those little buggers squirming around inside my body? I think not.

So why am I feeling this temptation to eat, drink, and be merry? It must be that red devil guy on my shoulder again. He's whispering: "Just because all the tourists have sensitive stomachs, does that mean you do?"

Maybe not. Maybe I'm special.

Besides, all the food looks and smells so good.

I dance over to the tables and eat and drink a little bit of everything in sight. Tacos stuffed with mashed potatoes in a smoky sauce. Tamales in real corn husks. The famous chicken in mole sauce, made with chocolate and chiles and lots of secret ingredients. Mango salad with hot peppers.

At this point I check to make sure Gran is still busy dancing her happy heart out. She is. I move on to bright pink pudding with multicolored sprinkles. Cake called *tres leches,* made with three kinds of milk. Fresh strawberries drizzled with cream. Coconut-papaya water.

Once in a while I catch Lili watching her dad and I see sadness in her eyes like a shadow. She loves him so much. It won't be easy for her to see him go.

Gran and I party on until the last folks leave at three in the morning, wishing Señor Sanchez and his brothers good luck in Michigan. Then I crash in my penthouse bed.

"I'm not feeling too well," I tell Gran when I wake up at noon. I don't mention my little piggy fest.

"You didn't drink water from the faucet, did you?" she

asks, testing my forehead for a fever. "Or eat strawberries or pudding at the fiesta?"

I shrug. Señorita Innocence.

By sunset I'm Señorita Sickie, and I'm in the emergency room at El Espíritu Hospital. My hands and feet are bloated and my stomach is as big as a baby whale. I can't keep food down. I hate to have to tell you this, but I have major diarrhea. Don't even try to talk to me, because my mouth is so dry and puckered, I can't talk back.

"You have amoebas," the doctor says. "And salmonella."

"Am I going to die?" I whine, forcing my swollen tongue to move. I hardly recognize my thick, slow voice.

"Would I let you die?" the doctor asks, raising his eyebrows. I think he's a little insulted. I shake my head no, and then tears start rolling down my cheeks because I'm supposed to be waiting for my call to go be a movie star and I'm supposed to be starting my new school. Now I'm nothing but a sick, bloated baby beluga with electric orange hair.

They want to keep me overnight in the hospital. I hear Gran talking quietly to the doctor. I lie on the exam table, lonely and miserable.

The saddest thoughts start washing over me: Why did Dad leave Mom? Is he ever coming back? If I fall in love someday, I want it to be forever. How could you give your heart to somebody and then suddenly, after you're married for fifteen years, just walk out?

Tears are flooding my face. Gran has to bring me a bunch of tissues because my nose is all clogged.

"It's okay, *tesoro*," she says sweetly. "The doctor will let you come home as long as you stay in bed for a few days."

I close my eyes and smile because I'm going home. I feel my dad holding my hand like when I was little. I can hear him singing that "Chim Chim Cher-ee" song from *Mary Poppins,* the one where the chimney sweep says he's lucky as lucky can be. I secretly thought my dad was telling me how lucky he felt to have me for a daughter.

The next thing I know I'm awake and I have no idea if it's midnight or six in the morning. I feel weak and dizzy. And swollen and sore.

I'm in Mexico, in my Rapunzel tower, I tell myself. It's as if I'm telling myself a story because my mind can't grasp that my body is such a mess. A truckload of parasites in teeny sombreros are throwing a fiesta in my body. But I'm going to be in a movie. Maybe. And I'm starting school in a Diego Rivera castle. Maybe.

The stars hang like fuzzy Christmas ornaments through the skylights. There's a crack in the black sky. Is it just the clouds opening to show a slit of a moon? Or is it a real crack? What if the crack gets bigger and something flies out of it? Like a ghost?

Leaves rustle against the window, making shadows wander across my bed. Where's Farley? I feel around in the covers until I find him. In my arms, he's so cuddly and he makes me feel safe.

I squint and look around me, trying to get my bearings. By the open window is my photo of Dad and Mom and me in a wood frame. We're smiling in the July snow at Rocky Mountain National Park. Our last vacation. Me and Mom and Dad...over.

I hear a rustling and a jingle-jangle sort of tinkling outside. Do ghosts make tinkling sounds? Then I remember we have chimes there, hanging from the avocado tree.

But wait! They're made of wood. Those chimes don't tinkle.

Is it *la fantasma?*

I lie dead still, crushing Farley against me. My mouth is too dry to holler for Gran. The jingle-jangle is out there again. I can't tell if it's in the yard or out on the street. It's the middle of the night. Why would someone be outside walking around?

"Gran!" I try to call, but my voice squeaks, a thin note from a broken clarinet. I'm shivering like it's the dead of winter. Why would the ghost want to get me? Because I've been snooping. Snooping where I don't belong.

Whatever the secret is, I won't tell! I'll delete the files. I'll rip up the printouts.

I don't want to know the old man and Veronica's secrets, I swear. I just want the ghost to go away and leave me alone.

Crash! The framed picture of my family in the snow falls off the table and hits the floor tiles.

It shatters into pieces.

# 15
# Daffodils

I'm here, Hayley. I'm coming!" Gran must have heard the crash. I hear her footsteps rushing up the spiral stairs. I'm huddled deep in the bed with Farley when she reaches me. She kisses my forehead, which she says is burning up with fever. Then she goes around closing all the open windows.

"That darned wind!" she says, picking up the photograph. The frame is split and the glass is in fragments. "No harm done," says Gran. "The photo is fine. We'll get a new frame for it tomorrow."

I want to tell her that a new frame won't fix what's really broken. My family. But I can't talk. I can only whimper and feel hot tears trickling out of the corners of my eyes, down into my ears.

"First I'm giving you more medicine," says Gran, pulling up a chair and giving me some pills. She reaches for the bottle of water beside my bed. There are new roses there. Yellow this time.

"I'm afraid, Gran," I admit. "I'm so scared."

"You're delirious with fever, sweetheart," she says. "If it keeps up, we'll have to put you in a cool bath."

Brrr. No thanks. I'm freezing already.

"Maybe it's a good time for a story," she suggests, taking a piece of drippy ice from the bowl and rubbing it across my neck. There's nothing in the world I'd like more than Gran's storytelling voice right now. I already feel calmer.

"When a butterfly first emerges from its chrysalis," she begins, "it's very vulnerable. Its wings are wet, all crushed up like expensive velvet. It takes a while for it to pump the blood from its warm, fuzzy body into its fragile wings."

I feel my brain relax. The wind begins to sound softer, like a butterfly in flight.

"Eventually those wings sprout like angel wings, and off that butterfly flies. It soars into the skies..." Farley feels extra-plush, and I'm getting warm and fuzzy myself. Gran soothes me into sweet dreams.

Day by day I get a little better. I have to sleep most of the time and drink gallons of some kind of sweet bottled water when I'm awake. Lying in bed, dozing and waking, I have way too much time to think about *la fantasma*. But I try to push that thought right out of my mind.

"How many days until school starts?" I ask every morning. It's six, then five, then four.

"You'll be fine by then," says Gran.

"Did Jorge call?" I ask every evening.

"No," says Gran.

"You'd tell me if he did, wouldn't you?"

"Of course I would, darlin'," she says.

On one of my sick days, Gran tosses me a movie magazine with Alonzo Luna on the cover. I read it so many times that I've memorized whole paragraphs in Spanish.

My fourth day in bed, Gran brings up my paints and a board to lay across my knees.

"We don't want those little parasite buggers to keep you from painting." She sets up everything right within my reach.

"There!" she says when the brushes and water glass and paints and paper are all in place. "Just like Frida Kahlo. She painted in bed after her accident, remember?"

I do remember. She painted some of her best work lying there with her legs completely paralyzed.

For some reason I want to paint daffodils. Maybe because I've been thinking so much about Mom. When I was little, Dad would bring her daffodils. I loved their faint, green scent, especially in early spring when we still had snow on the ground. I know Mom sometimes still hopes Dad will show up one of these days at the door with a handful of daffodils.

Sam's been sending me get-well e-mails that Gran prints and brings to me. Sam's making fun of my Mexican bug infestation. She starts her notes with "Dear Frankintestines." Mom's been calling every day. By the fifth day, I'm out of bed and dressed in jeans. My bloated belly is almost back to normal.

"I'm so much better," I tell Mom when she calls.

"You know what?" she says. "So am I, sweetie. A little better every day."

I believe her. I just don't mention anything about how I've been painting daffodils.

# 16

## B is for Bronco

Somewhere in the back of my brain I had the idea that I would basically be taking a semester off, breezing my way through some fun, lightweight classes. I pictured myself spending my days reading and pondering life like a princess in a castle who's surrounded by Diego Rivera murals.

Reality check! If my first day is any indication, school is going to be hard, hard, hard. These Mexican teachers expect you to be very studious (which I am), to be punctual (whatever happened to laid-back Mexican time?), and not to fool around (which I sometimes enjoy doing). Plus, they give you a heavy-duty load of homework.

I'm in second-level Spanish, and my teacher Señor Torres says his plan is to drill verbs into my head until I can actually carry on a halfway intelligent conversation with anybody I meet on the street. He wears a coat that's just a tad too tight in the shoulders and a tad short at the cuffs, with a dull tie and shiny loafers. He has a carved wooden pointer that he waves around like he's an orchestra conductor.

"Señorita Margarita, give me the imperfect conjugation of *jugar,*" he orders, aiming his wand at my nose. Don't shoot! I think.

*Jugar* means "to play." I wish I *could* play. This is far from it. You've heard of past, present, and future tenses. Well, Spanish has more verb tenses than I've ever heard names for: conditional, past perfect, imperfect. And that's only a few in store for me. Yikes!

Even art is intense. My *maestro,* Señor Garcia Garcia, is teaching me to paint from my imagination, and to make a big mess while I'm at it. He says to paint from the heart—*del corazón.* He punctuates the last two words by slapping himself on the chest over his heart. Today I painted a vase full of baby pink roses. It was all neat and perfect. I liked it. He didn't.

"You are not painting, Señorita Margarita," Señor Garcia told me, all passionate and dramatic as he passed by my easel. "You are illustrating."

Señor Garcia is a big man who looks like Pancho Villa, the revolutionary, with a thick mustache and eyes like chocolate, ready to melt.

"If you want to study in my class, *señorita,* you must put *yourself* onto the canvas. Your emotions. Your *corazón.*"

I have to finish an entire painting, from beginning to end, in one month. And I have to put my heart—*mi corazón*—onto the canvas, to boot. If you're any kind of artist, you know how hard this is going to be. How do you find what's in your heart? And then pick colors to match?

Oh, but guess who's in painting class with me? Bronco. The *muy guapo* guy who let me in the door on my visit here with Gran. He's cute and he's cheery, too. There's red and yellow and purple paint under his fingernails and there are paint splatters all over his clothes. His paintings are awesome, by the way. Loaded with color, like a fiesta.

One leetle problem: Bronco doesn't speak much English. I expect that Señor Torres will be pleased to see me working industriously to get all those Spanish verbs conjugated.

Now we come to dance class. Wouldn't you think it would be a cinch? No way! Every step in a traditional dance has a purpose and conveys some symbolic meaning. We do the Corn Dance first, the dance for a good harvest. You have to move like a deer and an eagle and a jaguar and a snake, and in between you spin around to face north, south, east, and west, stomping a certain way.

The Mexican kids really get into it. Manuel gels his hair into a Mohawk just for class. Gustavo takes out a mirror and paints a black mask across his eyes. And that's fine with Señorita Murillo, our teacher. Can you imagine anyone allowing that back in Kalamazoo? Señorita Murillo insists that you get into the jaguar-deer-snake-eagle spirit of it all. She believes you need to do whatever it takes to dance the dance.

I believe I need to do whatever it takes not to fall on my butt, which I have a tendency to do.

One thing about dance class: It definitely has the largest number of cute *muchachos*. Gustavo is cute, and Manuel is cute, and then there are José, Roberto, Ricardo... Enough for now. Bronco's still my fave, although unfortunately he's not in this class.

The Corn Dance is as far as we get today. The other classes, in brief:

Math is great because Lili sits next to me. Plus, I'm good at fractions, which is what we work on today. Math is the same no matter what language you learn it in. But geography is a different story! Here they teach that there are six continents, not seven. To them, North and South America are one and the same, and they simply call it "America."

Mexican history is the hardest of all, even though it's only us *gringos* in the class. None of us knows one thing about Mexican presidents or Mexican wars, Mexican writers or Mexican social activists. We all sit staring at our hands in our laps when Señor Aragon asks questions. I'm worried I might not make it through this one.

"I'll help you," Lili tells me on the walk home.

"Thanks," I say.

"So which way do we turn to get home?" I ask her. I have no clue.

"Toward the library," she says.

"And which way is the library?" I ask her.

"Why don't you practice your Spanish? Ask somebody." Lili has a big smile on her face. "It'll be good for you!"

Yeah, dandy. But I know she's right. It's a breeze getting around San Miguel when I've got Lili to speak for me. Okay, here goes. I see a lady wearing a turquoise shawl and a long pink and lime green skirt, the way I used to think everybody dressed here when I was back in the U.S.

"*¿Por favor, donde está la biblioteca?*" I ask her. I'm feeling *muy* proud that my two years of Kalamazoo Spanish classes have made me sound pretty darned good.

*"Esmuycercanecessitasolamenteiralisquierzaala-esquinaydespuesvaaverla,"* she rattles off in response.

Whoa!

*"Muchas gracias, señora,"* I say, turning to walk away.

She chuckles pleasantly, puts her hands on my shoulders, and spins me in the right direction. I feel like an idiot, but she couldn't be nicer. I head the right way and Lili follows behind me, giggling her head off.

# 17
# Bring on the Bulls!

**E**xhilarating!" Gran cries, tossing her red shawl over her shoulder. It's Running of the Bulls day. There are four bulls—real bulls, horns and all—stampeding through the streets around the San Miguel square. Right in front of the church! Crowds of rowdy people in the street push against each other, yelling and screaming. Most of them are wearing red bandanas tied around their necks for the occasion.

Basically what happens is that the townspeople—mostly older boys and men—leap in front of the bulls, then race like crazy, hoping to outrun them and not get gored in the meantime. It's a mini version of the famous Running of the Bulls, which takes place in Pamplona, Spain, every summer.

"Come on, Gran, let's get out of here," I say. "Too many people. Too much violence. I don't want to watch some kid get stabbed by a horn."

"Just one more look-see!" says Gran. If you ask me, she's a little too caught up in all this madness. I'm worried. She pushes her way to the edge of the street. Just then one of the raging beasts storms into the crowd. We leap back, along with about a hundred other stunned onlookers. Gran just misses getting pierced by the horn of a charging bull.

"This is way too dangerous!" I shout over the chaos. "Come on, Gran!"

I hook her arm in mine and practically drag her through the mob, away from the *Jardín*. My heart is pounding a mile a minute. I'm scared she's going to want to head right back into the action.

"Let's have a *limonada*," I say. "We can't see anything from here anyway. Too many people, Gran."

"Wait till I tell Oliver!" Gran exclaims, catching her breath. She's leaning against a rosy terra-cotta building to steady her shaking legs. "I never imagined I'd ever be chased by an angry two-thousand-pound bull!"

Oliver is my grandpa. I never met him, though, because he died before I was born. Gran almost never calls him Oliver. It's always "your grandpa." It must be the excitement of her close call.

I take Gran to a *cantina* that has a balcony with a view of the *Jardín* craziness below. I'm a whole lot more upset than she seems to be.

*"Dos limonadas, por favor,"* I tell the waiter. A couple of limeades to refresh us both.

"It's safer watching it from here, I suppose," says Gran, chuckling. She picks up the menu to use as a fan.

"That was insane, Gran. And I don't ever want to see you doing anything like that again." I speak to her like she's the kid and I'm the grandma. I don't want to lose Gran. And certainly not in some gory death, poked in the gut by a bull.

"We all saw you down there with the bulls, *señora*," a man tells Gran in Spanish. He's sitting at the bar with a bunch of other men. He tells her she almost lost her life. "Let me buy you a beer," he offers.

Of course, I expect Gran to say No, thank you.

But I hear *"¡Excelente! ¡Gracias!"* coming out of her mouth. I'm shocked.

When Gran's cold beer arrives, she takes a long swig and sits back in her chair, fanning herself. She starts giving the men at the bar a detailed description of her near-death story. They love it. They shake their heads like she's a lunatic for getting that close to the wild bulls.

They used to run with the bulls when they were young and stupid, they tell her. But at her age?

They're treating her like some kind of heroine in a movie. I'm not happy about this. At all.

"How about we go home for a game of Scrabble?" I suggest. I've never known Gran to turn down a game of Scrabble.

"Bring the *abuelita* another beer!" calls a man in a huge-brimmed cowboy hat.

*"¡Gracias, señor!"* says Gran happily. The cowboy saunters over with Gran's beer and they start chatting like good old friends.

Fine. No Scrabble.

When I get to be seventy, am I going to behave like this? After two beers I insist that we go home. That night, we lie on my bed and watch fireworks through the skylight.

*"Tesoro,"* Gran says, "we have to conserve our energy, because another fiesta starts tomorrow!"

Another fiesta? Wow, autumn is very different here than it is in Kalamazoo. At home fall feels quiet and serious. You start back to school and spend hours in the library. There's a brisk chill in the air. The leaves turn red and orange and begin to fall.

It's not like that here. There are bright flowers everywhere and butterflies and spring birds. The summer rains stop and the air dries out. There's one fiesta after the next in San Miguel.

At midnight on September 16, we join the whole crowded town in the traditional shouting in the streets. This one is called *El Grito*—the shout for Mexican independence. The fiesta commemorates the time when Father Hidalgo held up a flag of the Virgin of Guadalupe and declared Mexico's independence from Spain. We read about it in our history class. In honor of the occasion, you shout *"¡Viva Mexico!"* for an hour straight with fireworks bursting over your head.

Then on October 12, there's a huge Columbus Day parade. But here in Mexico, the holiday is called *el Día de la Raza*. That means the Day of the Race, and on this occasion they celebrate the Hispanic heritage of all of Latin America.

The history of Mexico is told in the procession: how the ancient Indian tribes lived among the jaguars and wolves, how Columbus came, then how the Spanish conquistadors arrived, and soon Catholic bishops with red hats. There are also devils and angels and twelve-foot-high Grim Reaper puppets.

Most of the kids in Señorita Murillo's class are dancing. They all look completely wild, wearing feather head-dresses or fringed jaguar pants or devil masks. Some dancers carry genuine dead ravens to symbolize the magic that was lost when the Europeans came.

I watch, hypnotized by the intensity of the dancers. Bronco twirls, his gold and turquoise Aztec cape flying like satin wings behind him. In his Indian costume, he's so *guapo,* I have to catch my breath.

"Next time, you will dance with them," says Señora Sanchez, coming up to wrap her arm around me. She tells me that November 20 is *el Día de la Revolución* parade. She's sewing *danza* costumes for a bunch of people in our neighborhood, including her kids. She wants me to join them.

"You mean it's okay if I'm not Mexican?" I ask her. She looks at me like I'm *loca,* a little nutty.

"Why would that make a difference?" she asks, frowning dramatically. "You can dance, *sí?*"

"Um, sort of. Kinda. I guess so."

She gives me a jolly pat on the back. "*Sí,* Margarita. On November 20, you will dance!"

# 18

# Painting Mi Corazón

For the Revolution Day parade, Lili and I will be jaguars. Most people call them *tigres* here, even though tigers have stripes and jaguars have spots. Anyway, the *chicos* will be wolves. Señora Sanchez shows us how to collect little dried fruits from a special tree at their house, fasten them together, and tie them to our ankles and wrists. They make a rattle-rattle sound every time we take a step.

Even though it's only October, we're preparing ahead of time. Today I decide to practice my wild beast look. Standing in front of the mirror, I rub spots of black and white and brown across my cheeks with makeup sticks. I dab jaguar blotches along my neck and arms and fill them in with brown. I ring my eyes in gold. I look so fierce, I'm scaring myself.

With my makeup on, I head outside to start that painting I'm supposed to bring to class in two weeks. I want to paint everything in this jungle garden, all the reds and hot pinks and magentas. The way the sun shines bright yellow on the stone pillars. The scarlet-orange bougainvillea. The cobalt blue bench. It's so incredibly beautiful here. I've never seen anything like it in my whole life.

I squeeze little puddles of color out of every tube and go into a mini painting frenzy. I start with the stones, bricks, fountain, stairways, and archways, using splashy colors, not grays and browns. Then I add flowers, fruits, leaves, and butterflies. After a couple of hours, I stand back and look.

I'm all splattered with paint on top of my jaguar spots, but I don't care. Señor Garcia would be proud. I'm taking his advice and am just trying to paint, paint, paint. I have an amazing feeling: I think I'm really beginning to be a painter!

Now when I squint at my canvas, I imagine I see Mexican fathers working in the fields, just beyond the stone arch. So I get back to work and paint them in.

I think of my house in Michigan and pretty soon it's in the background, too. Out of nowhere I picture a bouquet of daffodils lying on the front step. Whoosh! I sweep on thick yellow paint to make them appear. Now I see a cluster of pumpkins sitting on the blue bench. With a few orange strokes—magic!

I think I'll name my painting *Kalamazoo, Mexico*. It's definitely a mixture of both places.

Just then the doorbell rings. I don't want to be interrupted, but I don't want to be rude, either. I open the door with a paintbrush between my teeth, like a rose.

It's Lili. She smiles at my jaguar face, but it's not her usual easy smile. Something's wrong. She says she has bad news about the dads.

I bring her in to the blue bench under the lime trees and she tells me the whole story.

Instead of the dads sending money home to their

families, she says the opposite is happening. Señora Sanchez and the other wives are having to send *them* money in Michigan for food and medicine.

"What do you mean?" I ask.

"They're not getting paid," she says.

There's some problem with the farm boss—*el dueño,* Lili calls him—and he can't pay them for a few more weeks. He's lending them money to get food, but they'll have to pay interest on the food loans, and in the meantime they have no cash to send home.

"That's so unfair! They should call a lawyer," I tell Lili. She shakes her head.

"Not possible," she says. "Some of the other farm workers do not have green cards."

"You need green card visas to work in the U.S., right?" I ask. "Then how did those other people get into the U.S.? The Border Patrol will only let you in to work if you have a green card."

"I know," says Lili. "They got to Michigan illegally. They paid a coyote."

"A coyote?" Obviously the word must mean something else in Spanish.

"A coyote is a man who sneaks people across the U.S. border. You pay him money and he finds a place where there are no guards that night. When he tells you to run, you run, and you keep on running until you get to a town where you can find work."

"Whoa. That sounds dangerous," I say.

"It is," says Lili. "Some people get shot by border police. Other people drown in the Rio Grande River while they are trying to swim across."

"That's terrible!"

"But they go because they need to earn money for their families," says Lili. "And only some people can get green cards from the U.S. government."

"So if the legal dads make trouble, the illegal men will get caught," I say, trying to get everything straight.

"That's right," Lili agrees. "Papa does not want that."

"Well, what else can be done? Could they just stop their work and go on strike until they get paid?" I ask.

"The *dueño* will just replace them with other workers," Lili points out.

"Let's see..." I'm chewing on the end of my paintbrush, trying to think of something that might help. "Maybe your dad and uncles should just come home now before it gets worse," I suggest.

I'm picturing Señor Sanchez sitting on the front stoop at night, laughing with his kids, twirling them over his head, playing soccer with a half-deflated ball. How terrible to think he's so far away and being treated badly.

"I'll talk to Gran," I say. "She always has good ideas."

"*Gracias,* Margarita," says Lili, hugging me tight.

"Are you going to the San Martín school tomorrow?" I ask her. Our geography teacher is driving us to a nearby ranch town to meet the elementary students.

"That's only for you *gringos,*" she says, smiling at the word. "You will like the children. They are very sweet."

"Too bad you can't come, too," I say.

"But you are going to talk to them about life in the United States, yes? I've never been there, so I would not be very helpful."

"You could come if your mom drives a group," I suggest.

"Our teacher is looking for one more volunteer car, since there are three schools."

"Margarita, we don't have a car," Lili reminds me.

"Oh, right," I say, wishing I had kept my mouth shut.

I walk Lili out to Parakeet Street and say hi to Señora Sanchez. *"Tigre,"* she says, gently pinching my painted cheek. "You make a good jaguar." There are dark circles under her eyes. Lili's mother must have been crying a lot. I sure wish I could do something to make everything all better.

# 19
## Dirt Poor

The next day Señorita Vasquez piles all of her geography students in cars, five in each, and off we zoom on our "educational outing." We're all dressed in jeans and T-shirts, just as she instructed. Each car is going to a different *rancho* school to talk to the students about what it's like to live in the U.S.

We drive down one narrow road after another for almost an hour with no traffic except men with burros and women with baskets of chiles. There's brown dust everywhere and shacks and half-built houses with dirt for floors.

Then we come to a little school in the middle of nowhere. Somebody from Texas gave the community money to build it. There was enough to pay for glass windows, doors with locks, electricity for lights in all three classrooms, and a kitchen so the kids can eat even if there's no food at home.

A teacher tells us the good news: they just got money to build two indoor bathrooms. In the meantime, however, there are no *baños*. And of course I have to pee.

The teacher tells me to go over to a stone wall in the

fields. Behind it is nothing but a row of smelly holes in a dirt floor. I glance around to make sure nobody's snooping and eventually I sort of figure out what to do. I'm really glad I had a napkin in my pocket from breakfast.

The *rancho* kids are excited to have visitors. My assignment is to pair up with a girl named Heather from California and talk to the first, second, and third grades combined.

Their teacher asks the class in Spanish how many of them have dads or brothers or uncles who are in the United States working right now. More than half the hands go up. The kids are very cute, and they all look eager to learn about the big country to their north.

Heather and I huddle together for a quick discussion. We sure don't want to tell the kids about malls and video games and wall-to-wall carpeting. That would make us feel like jerks.

So we talk about farms, which the kids know more about than we do. Every day their dads pull weeds, kill bugs, and irrigate the fields with water from lakes and rivers. They get up early so they're in the fields when the sun comes up. That gives me an idea.

I tell them the sky is pink and orange at sunrise in the United States.

"It is in Mexico, too!" they all shout. And they understood what I said in Spanish—I'm thrilled!

Heather tells them that every day their dads see the same sunrise that the kids see here in Mexico.

"*¿La misma?* The same?" they ask.

"*Sí,*" I tell them. "*La misma.* The same." They're so happy about that.

A girl named Maria wants to tell us all about her dad and the pumpkins.

She says in Spanish that her papa is in Wisconsin. Sometimes in September there is an early snow and the men have to work all night.

Another boy cuts in. He tells us that they use the headlights from trucks to light up the fields.

Pretty soon the whole class is adding on bits and pieces of the story. It's the same deal in Illinois and North Carolina and Colorado. The dads work fast, cutting, picking, tossing, filling trucks, unloading, and stacking pumpkins in barns and garages to keep them safe from freezing. If they don't get everything picked, the frost will kill all the pumpkins.

Heather finishes the group story. After they work for twenty-four hours straight, she tells them, the men are tired, but very, very proud. They save the farmer's whole pumpkin crop.

The kids cheer and clap because their dads are heroes. I personally don't know anybody in Kalamazoo who treats the migrant workers like heroes. Maybe when I get home, I should try to find out how the Mexican workers are really treated.

I tell them that when the men are not busy working, they miss their families and can't wait to come home.

One girl asks what happens if they find new families in the United States. She says Pulga's dad went to Texas and never came back.

Pulga is a short, spunky, sweet-looking kid. His nickname means "flea." It really gets to me when I look at him. A dad who left and never came back. Just thinking about dads leaving makes my throat start closing up.

The kids' eyes are bright and wide, waiting for me to answer since I'm the *gringa*. I'm from Michigan. I should know everything there is to know about grapes and blueberries and apples and pumpkins and migrant workers and life in the U.S., right?

"That doesn't happen very often," I say quickly, as if I know what I'm talking about. I wish I could give them a fairy-tale ending. Their lives are hard enough. They don't even have bathrooms, for crying out loud.

I gulp back tears, relieved when the bell rings. We're done. A small army of kids leads us up the farm road, skipping alongside the car. The teachers and some of the moms have set up a table with chicken-filled tortillas and cold cans of Coke for us. They come out to shake our hands and hug us when we leave.

I can see how poor they are. But they don't act poor. They act like the most generous people I've ever met.

*"Gracias,"* they tell us over and over. "Thank you for visiting the children."

When I get home I feel a new painting itching at me. I head straight out to my sanctuary.

What am I feeling? I cut another piece of Sam's nice canvas and stretch it over a wood frame.

What am I thinking? I staple the canvas and paint it with plain white house paint, which is what they use at school instead of something fancy.

What's gnawing at my soul?

These are the questions Señor Garcia would ask.

Dads. That's what's gnawing at me.

Lili's dad. Pulga's dad. My dad.

Lili's dad is in big trouble in Michigan, which is home for me and a strange, foreign place for him. He's just trying to earn some money for his family—legally—and then come back and sell his birds again. He has a green card. I know he's a hard worker. But some nasty boss won't even give him his pay.

And then there's my dad, who would probably say that selling birds isn't work. It's a hobby. To work, you have to put on a suit and go to an office. He'd tell Lili's dad to get back to Mexico and get a real job.

Pulga's dad is gone and starting a new family somewhere else. *Malo.* Bad. Bad, bad, bad.

While I've been thinking, I've been painting big rock walls. I've painted spiky barbed wire along the top. Painting walls...what's that about?

Now I start seeing words as if they're appearing on the canvas. I grab a thin brush and black paint. I scribble words here and there:

*"Niños. Padres."* Children. Fathers.

"Open Your Eyes."

"We Are All *Americanos.*"

"No North America. No Central or South America. One continent."

Words start bursting all along the edge of the frame: "No Borders, No Borders, No Borders."

I'm painting as fast as I can, whatever *mi corazón* is telling me to paint. I don't even know why I'm writing this stuff.

If I were God I would make everything perfect from beginning to end. Everybody would love to stay married. Everybody would have plenty of money so they wouldn't have to leave their families to go earn it. Everybody would pay workers on time. Everybody all over the world would understand each other. Nobody would hate anybody else. Amen.

# 20
## Moth Broth Night

H ow's that moth broth coming?" Gran calls.

"Just hunky-dory," I holler back.

Lili and I are in the kitchen stirring up a goopy mess of peaches, sugar, and water that's been rotting for two days. It's Gran's special "moth" formula.

"They come from far and wide when they get a whiff of that broth!" she told us.

You'd think Gran was a butterfly herself the way she's flitting around. She's pulling out flashlights and bed-sheets, and she's blissfully happy. Why? Because lately our yard has gotten more jungle-like than ever. In a buggy way.

As soon as the rainy season ended, the scorpions started creeping out from between the rocks. Don't ask. And there are slugs, too, slugs the size of cheese puffs. Four snuck in under the screen door and crawled around our front room floor last night. Good thing for them Gran loves all living things. She just picks up the slugs, talks sweetly to them, and puts them outside, away from the house.

So tonight is Gran's big night—Moth Night. We used to do moth nights in Michigan, too. Gran makes a tent out of white sheets and puts a black light inside. We camp out overnight in the tent to watch moths come flying from miles away.

"They call them 'night butterflies' here," says Gran, hammering a stake into the ground for the tent. *"Mariposas nocturnales."*

Whatever. I just call them bugs with wings. Most moths come in woody colors with designs that match the tree bark, so you can't possibly say they're as pretty as butterflies. Plus their bodies are chubby and fuzzy. Yuck!

The phone rings and I talk to my mom while I smear moth broth onto the trunks of the lime and avocado trees. Lili's sugaring up the pillars by the *casita* door.

"Guess what, sweetie?" my mom asks me. I hold my breath since I'm not sure what's up.

"I'm going back to school," she announces.

Back to school? Is this good? Is this bad?

Next Monday Mom is going to start studying culinary arts. She wants to be a chef. Actually she's always loved cooking, so I'd say this is a very good thing.

"That's so great, Mom," I tell her. I love the lively spark in her voice. I pray for a *milagro*—that the spark will last.

"Enough about me," my mom says then. "Tell me about Lili. And the movie...Oh, and how's your art?"

I'm afraid to tell her much because I'm suspicious she might just say, "How nice, honey" in that hollow way. Then that hole in my gut will show up again.

"It's all fine," I say cautiously. There's a long pause. Then Mom talks.

"Really, Hayley. Tell me everything. I know I've been checked out for a while. But I'm coming back. I think about you every day, honey. I want to know all about what you're doing."

Whoa. This is new.

I tell her about Lili and the movie costumes and Mr. Sanchez having trouble on the vineyard in Michigan.

"They're here near Kalamazoo?" she asks. "Maybe I can help somehow."

She sounds like she means it.

"That's really nice, Mom," I tell her. "Thanks."

When I hang up I'm thrilled that Mom sounds so much better. I'm also pretty excited about her offer to help the workers, but I'm afraid to get my hopes up too far. Could Mom really help? Lately she's hardly been able to help herself. But it's pretty cool she's going to go back to school.

"People can change," Gran tells me. "It's like a caterpillar emerging from a cocoon. Once it turns into a butterfly, or a moth, there's no going back."

It's like one of Gran's miracles. My feet are doing a little dance and I'm suddenly enjoying the moth paint job. Before long dark sets in. We climb into the tent, and it's just plain magical. Lili and I watch the gargantuan moth shadows appear like dark, buggy ghosts and land on the outside of the white tent.

Pretty soon the tent is peppered with moths. All three of us crawl outside to take a good look at their wings because from inside you can't see the markings, just their silhouettes.

Some are big as both my hands. Some have eyeball patterns on their wings to protect them from hungry birds. I can't imagine wanting to chow down on those fat, fuzzy bodies, but then again, I'm not a bird.

"Look! A luna!" whispers Gran. She's pointing to a pale green moth with long tails. "I can't believe it."

"Luna, as in Alonzo Luna?" I whisper back. Lili giggles.

"Exactly," says Gran. "*Luna* means moon, of course. It almost glows like the moon, doesn't it?"

It looks luminescent, with white full moons on its wings.

"Lunas don't usually fly this far south. What an honor!" whispers Gran, totally awestruck.

After checking out all the night visitors, we go back in the tent for a while. I make sure there are no scorpions glowing under the black light. The coast is clear. Lili tunes her radio to soft guitar music. Gran has fixed us popcorn balls and taffy apples, which taste just like Halloween back home in Kalamazoo.

Soon we're wrapped up in our sleeping bags like a trio of cozy caterpillars. Outside the moths flit and wave their wings to the music, dancing an autumn ballet. We lie there talking about big things and little things. How Lili and I are moving from one stage of life into the next, from twelve to thirteen. How we think some words—like "phlegm"—are impossible to spell when you're trying to learn English. How maybe since Mom is brave enough to go to cooking school, it's time for Gran to give her that secret sweet-and-spicy mango salsa recipe. That would help to keep her on her toes!

Then Gran says, straight out of the blue, "I think the ghost might be back again."

I feel like I just got struck by a lightning bolt. We both

sit straight up at the same time, staring at Gran.

"You know about the ghost?" I say, my voice rising to a squeak. "You *saw* the ghost? I thought you didn't believe in such things." Lili and I move closer together, touching shoulders.

"Well, there was definitely an unhappiness in this house when I first moved in," Gran says. "I thought it was gone, but I felt it again the other night. A cold wash of sadness that blew through."

"Weren't you afraid, Gran?" I ask. Me, I'd be shaking in my Mexican rhinestone sandals.

"No, no, I wasn't afraid. I'm not the one who's a lost ghost."

"So how do you rid your home of this *fantasma?*" Lili asks. Good question.

"I'm not sure," says Gran.

"We could bring in a *curandera,*" Lili suggests.

"What's that?" I ask.

A *curandera,* it turns out, is a sort of spirit healer who usually works with people, but also talks to ghosts. She uses herbs and grasses and stones and natural things to help ghosts move on to a peaceful place.

Why didn't Lili tell me this before?

"After you die you must leave this earth," Lili explains. "You can come back for a little visit now and then if you are invited by someone who loves you."

"So ghosts come back to visit? People ask them to come?" Creepy.

"No, not ghosts," says Gran. "Ghosts and spirits are two different things. Spirits like your Grandpa Oliver are settled. Happy."

I knew that Gran talked to my grandpa all the time. But it turns out that Grandpa comes back to visit Gran now and again. When she needs advice. Or a little hug. Is it me, or is this a *very* weird concept?

"Ghosts are a whole other thing," Gran says. "They have unfinished business. They hang around, wanting things on earth to be different from the way they really turned out. Once they can face the truth, they happily move to the spirit world."

Maybe it's the same for us living people, I think. We're happier if we just quit pretending things are different than they are. If we just face the truth.

"Maybe we'll hire a *curandera*," Gran says.

Lili explains to us that if the ghost is really bad we'll have to bring in a shaman, a more powerful medicine man or medicine woman.

But Gran decides we'll try to tackle the ghost situation ourselves. Day of the Dead is coming on November 2. I don't know anything about it, but just the name of it scares the pants off me. A special day for the *dead?*

Lili agrees with Gran that the Day of the Dead would be a good time, so we set November 2 as the date for our secret ghostbuster plan. That's three whole days away. How am I supposed to sleep until then? What if the ghost gets me before we can bust him or her?

Gran switches off the light and settles into her sleeping bag. Even though I feel sure that I won't be able to sleep, I close my eyes. Just when Gran, deep in sleep, starts snoring a tiny bit, I hear the jingle-jangle tinkling noise again. I'm sure it's out on the street this time. Maybe it's at Lili's front door.

Lili turns her head. She hears it, too. The two of us are dead silent, staring into each other's eyes, not budging.

Then it's gone. Total silence except for the crickets and a street cat or two.

"Something's up," I whisper.

"I just hope that wasn't *la fantasma,*" Lili whispers back. "Do you think it heard us?"

We scoot our sleeping bags just a bit closer together and turn the flashlight back on for a night-light, just in case.

# 21
# Trick or Treat

I carve out a jagged, screaming mouth and toss it onto Gran's compost pile.

"*¡Feo!*" howls Lili. "Very ugly!"

"Almost as ugly as yours!" I tell her.

We're carving weird-shaped gourds to look like wicked little gremlins. We plan to put candles in them and hang them from the garden trees tonight to spook ourselves.

It's Halloween, but that's not such a big deal here in Mexico. We won't be trick-or-treating or wearing costumes or dunking for apples.

"Something wonderful happened at my house last night," Lili tells me as she gouges out a handful of gourd goo.

"*La fantasma* came for a visit?" I ask, teasing.

"Nooo. Something *mucho mejor,* much better. Someone pushed an envelope full of money under our door!"

"What? Who?" I ask.

"Who knows? The envelope had no writing on it," Lili says. "This is the third envelope in the past three months."

"Wow! That's amazing! There's a secret giver in the neighborhood!" I say.

I'm wondering if it was Gran. It would be just like her to do something generous and not say a word about it.

But Gran was asleep before we were last night.

"Remember the noise we heard that we thought might be the ghost?" I ask.

"Oooh...You don't think that...No," says Lili, her eyes wide.

"So whoever...or whatever...made those tinkly sounds..."

"...might have left the money," whispers Lili. "But the money is real pesos. Do ghosts have money?"

Good question. I don't think they *have* money in the spirit world. But can they steal money and then give it to somebody who needs it?

"We are sending the money up to Papa," Lili says.

"That's great," I say, nodding. Then I hear a very strange noise. "Lili, listen," I whisper. "Señora Bruja is singing to her pigs!" Humming, rather. She has a throaty hum, like our fake actress voices.

"She's *loca*," says Lili. "Crazy."

"Maybe she's getting ready to go flying off on her broom tonight," I suggest.

"That's a terrible thing to say," Lili tells me, giggling. "But funny!"

We both break into a silly witch cackle.

"So why do you think she hates people so much?" I ask.

"Why does anybody hate anybody?" says Lili, shrugging. "As they say: *Cada persona es un mundo.*"

"Every person is a world?" I translate. "I don't think we say that in English."

"Maybe in English it's more like 'Every individual is a separate world,'" says Lili. "Does that make sense?"

"Hmmm. Yeah, I guess so. Like, we can never know the real deal about someone like *la Bruja*. We don't know all of what's happened in her world."

"Exactly," says Lili. She sets her finished jack-o-lantern gourd in our pile on the blue bench. I add mine. That makes eight. Plenty.

"Let's take her a present," I say suddenly.

"Who?" asks Lili.

"*La Bruja*. Let's take her a gift."

"Why?" Lili looks confused.

"Just because. Because nobody ever gives her presents, I bet."

"That is a nice idea," Lili agrees. She starts looking around the yard for something to give.

"We could give her a gourd," she suggests.

"Too creepy," I say. "She'll think we're being mean."

"Well, maybe she would like some limes?"

Perfect! We start shaking the trunks of our trees. Ripe green limes come bumping and crashing down from the branches. We find an old basket in the shed and fill it up with our peace offering. Then we go next door and ring and knock. We can hear the neighborhood zoo clacking and barking and snorting in there.

But *la Bruja* doesn't answer her door. No big surprise.

Lili and I leave the limes on the stoop like secret givers and go back to visit our eight gourdy gremlins. They're way scarier than Halloween pumpkins since you can't cut them smoothly. They're ragged and rough and insane-looking.

"Wait till they're lit up tonight!" I threaten. "Eeek!"

"In the meantime, let's go downtown," Lili suggests. "You can see how we celebrate here in Mexico!"

"Is it kind of like our Halloween?" I ask.

"I don't think so. Not at all. Just come see," says Lili.

As we walk down Parakeet Street we hear slow, ancient music coming from the *Jardín*. There are marigold petals strewn all over the ground on every street.

"People drop the petals to make a path for the spirits to follow to San Miguel," Lili explains. I remember that Gran said spirits were *settled* ghosts.

We pass tables along the street piled with little sugar skulls and skeletons popping out of tiny sugar coffins. In front of the church artists are creating skull and bones paintings made of colored sand and flower petals. Everybody's very quiet.

"We celebrate for three days," says Lili. "If you like, you can come with my family on November 2. You can spend the night in the cemetery."

The cemetery! Why would I ever want to—?

Just then a butterfly lands on my shoulder. I'm happy to change the subject.

"Look!" I whisper. "A monarch!"

"Do you know about the monarchs?" Lili asks.

I know we have them in Michigan in the summer and that now they're migrating to Mexico for the winter. I've seen more monarch butterflies the past few days than I ever even knew existed.

"They start way up in Canada and the States and fly four thousand miles to get here," says Lili. "They end up at the same forests in Michaocan where all their ancestors have gone for centuries."

"How do they know the way?" I ask.

"It is a mystery," says Lili. "We call the monarchs *angelitos*."

"Little angels?" I ask her.

"Exactly. The monarchs are the spirits of children who died, coming back for a visit on the Day of the Dead—*el Día de los Muertos*."

My *angelito* leaves my shoulder, flying off to Michoacan, I suppose.

"Isn't that kind of sad, about the children visiting?" I ask.

"Not at all," says Lili. "We're all going to die. That's just a part of life."

"You've got a point there," I say. "I guess."

I don't want to think about dying. I mean, I've only been on this planet for twelve and a half years. I have a long way to go. I hope.

# 22
# Day of the Dead

H and me that photo, will you?" Gran asks. I pass her a picture of my grandpa dressed up like a vampire for Halloween. He's grinning at the camera while sucking on the throat of a rubber bat.

"Are you sure this is the one you want to use tonight?" I ask. I have to say, it's not very respectful of the dead, in my opinion.

"Absolutely," declares Gran, chuckling as she looks at the picture. "Your grandpa always made me laugh."

It's the first of November and time for the start of the Day of the Dead celebration. There's a big altar at the museum. For the altar you bring photos of people you loved who died. And souvenirs of things you miss about them. There will be a ceremony run by a Mexican healer.

"Is the healer the *curandera* you were talking about?" I ask. "The one who will get rid of the ghost?"

"We'll see," says Gran mysteriously. "But right now it's time to go shopping."

We head out to buy special things to honor Grandpa Oliver tonight. We buy a sugar skull with blue glitter eyes since blue was his favorite color. We buy little sugar enchiladas in red sparkle sauce. We go to the smoke shop where Gran gets a Cuban cigar, which apparently is very special.

"Once a year, every Christmas Eve, your grandpa would smoke one cigar, and it had to be the best!" she says. I can see that this Day of the Dead deal isn't sad for her. She loves remembering all the funny and quirky and sweet things about my grandpa.

"Did he like hot chocolate?" I ask. I'm checking out a mini cocoa cup on a mini sugar saucer with teensy yellow flowers somebody painted on by hand.

"He did," Gran tells me as sunbeams sparkle on her face through her straw hat. "He liked to sit by the fire with his cocoa on those snowy Michigan nights."

It takes us an hour to find just the perfect blue sugar cup with the darkest chocolate inside. On the way we spot some chocolate kisses.

"Oh, his favorite!" says Gran. "When he was sick at the end of his life I kept a bowl of them beside his bed. I'd unwrap one and pop it in his mouth. It made him smile."

After an afternoon of collecting Grandpa treats, we meet up with Lili's family and we all head for the museum. The sunset is purple-pink, and the whole town has turned into an eerie fantasy scene.

Candles and lanterns glow in doorways. Fluttering over our heads are banners of *papel picado,* which is paper with designs punched in it. The cut-out skulls and skeletons grin at us through bright-colored tissue paper.

Shop windows are packed with *calacas*—skeletons like Cynthia in Gran's front room. They're skeletons of every size, from teeny to ten feet tall, doing normal everyday things like cooking breakfast and riding bikes and playing violins. You can smell marigolds everywhere.

"The Aztecs believed marigolds were the flowers of the dead," Gran tells me. We stop and buy orange bouquets for our group and pretty soon we're our own procession. Me and Lili and Gran and Señora Sanchez and the *chicos* are all carrying marigold bouquets the size of small trees.

There are little altars here and there in honor of Diego Rivera, Frida Kahlo, Father Hidalgo, and other famous Mexican people I've been learning about in history class. I have to admit, if it weren't for Señor Aragon, none of this would make much sense to me.

We follow the crowd along the orange petal path and into the dark, cool rooms of the museum. The healer, who's wearing a bright caftan and beaded jewelry, is at the community altar. She explains that the dead will return—just for this one night—to visit us. Tonight *los angelitos,* the children, will come. Tomorrow night everyone else will visit.

A little chill creeps up my arms. But nobody around me seems to think this is the least bit spooky.

The big thing is that we have to show the spirits where to find us. There's a pot of incense burning so they can follow the scent of the smoke. There's guitar music they can hear. Of course, they can also see the field of bright orange marigolds we're all carrying.

Everyone turns to the east, south, west, then north to invite back the souls of those we loved. Soon people start putting souvenirs on the altar. There are photos and candles and sugar treats. Dolls and cigars. Cans of soda and bottles of tequila.

I see Lili staring in shock at a young woman ahead of us in the crowd.

"That's Angela," she whispers.

"Angela?" I ask. "You mean, the *haunted* Angela?"

Lili nods. Angela is setting a photo of a man on the altar along with a folded piece of paper.

"Veronica's father!" says Lili.

"What?" I ask.

"The man in the photo. It's the old man who died in your grandmother's house. I remember seeing that picture in the newspaper."

I squint to try to see his face. He just looks like an ordinary old man. What could he have possibly done that was so awful?

*"La fantasma?"* I whisper. My heart starts beating fast.

*"Sí,"* Lili says. "Our ghost."

# 23
# Ghost Story

The next thing I know I'm dashing out the door into the shadowy museum garden, following behind Angela, who is being dragged by Lili. Candles stuck in dried gourds flicker along the marigold path. Paper skull cutouts flutter over our heads.

"Do you remember me?" Lili asks Angela.

"Yes, I think so. You're...you were...my neighbor, *sí?*" Angela says. She seems confused. I can't say I blame her.

"Yes," says Lili. "And Veronica's neighbor."

"You know—knew—Veronica?" Angela asks, sounding shocked.

"We saw you put her father's picture on the altar," says Lili.

"I did," says Angela. "But how did you know he was her father?"

Lili and I exchange looks. We're not giving away any secrets.

"We want to know everything. About Veronica. Her father. *La fantasma,*" I say quietly. We don't have time to beat around the bush here. We've got to get all the information we can before this Angela disappears again. But we don't want to draw a crowd, either. This is very private stuff.

"Well..." Angela hesitates.

"Please," says Lili, giving her an imploring look.

"All right. Here, sit down a minute. I'll try to explain." Angela sits on a carved wooden bench. Lili and I sit on each side, sandwiching her in so she can't run off into the Day of the Dead night.

"Remember when I moved into Veronica's *casita?*" Angela asks Lili.

"Of course I do," says Lili.

"I found Veronica's computer that night," she says. "I read something I shouldn't have read."

"Her private files?" I ask. My hand flies right to my mouth. But it's too late. Now I have to explain how I also found the computer. And how Lili and I read the files left in the trash.

"Trash? I thought I got rid of everything!" says Angela.

*"You* got rid of everything?" I asked. "We thought *Veronica* tried to delete those files."

"No, it was me. Anyway, I'm talking about a different file. It was a folder called *Vaya con Dios.* Good-bye. Go with God."

"B...but...I didn't see one called that," I stammer.

"That's because I deleted it," Angela says quietly. "I printed it out, deleted the folder, and transferred all the other files to the trash bin. I meant to clear the trash, but I guess I forgot. Then I put the computer back the way I found it."

"And then?" asks Lili.

"Well, I was really shaken. I just had to get out of that *casita.*"

"Why? What was in the letter?" I ask.

Angela bites her lip. "I'm not sure it's something I should share." She sits there silently. Maybe we shouldn't push her too much right now. We can come back to the letter later.

"So tell us about the ghost pushing you down the spiral staircase," I say.

"Oh, that," says Angela. She looks away.

Lili frowns. "What do you mean?" she asks.

"I think Angela means she didn't tell the truth about the ghost," I say. "Is that right, Angela?" This young woman is really starting to make me mad.

Angela shrugs.

"After I read Veronica's letter, I got scared. I felt a sad, spiteful presence all around me. I had to get out of that house immediately."

"And then?" I ask. My voice is a little shaky.

"Then I raced up to the top floor and packed my things. As I came back downstairs..."

"Veronica's ghost pushed you from behind," I finish.

Angela shakes her head.

"The ghost of Veronica's father pushed you?" Lili tries.

"No." Angela sighs. "The truth is, I tripped and fell. Simple as that."

*What?* No ghost? After all this?

"I was lucky I only ended up with a bruised shoulder and a sore ankle," says Angela. "I should have been more careful. I knew that one step was cracked."

"But you told my mother it was the ghost who pushed you," says Lili.

"As I limped out the front door with my suitcases, your mother was standing there on the street. Had I felt a real presence? Hadn't I? I wasn't sure. But I wasn't going to tell her I'd read Veronica's letter."

"So?" I prod. When was Angela going to tell us about that letter? Sooner or later she was going to crack.

"So I had to say something. I was very shaken," says Angela. "I made up the story about the ghost pushing me."

Lili and I stare at Angela in silence.

"You lied," says Lili.

"Well, I thought that I had felt something...*maybe* a ghost...but as time went by, I realized it was probably my imagination," admits Angela. "Anyway, I lied and told your mother I was moving far, far away. I was so scared. But I ended up only moving to the other side of town."

Huh? I don't get it. If there was no ghost, why was Angela so scared? Because she lied to Lili's mother? I'm sure that Señora Sanchez would understand if she explained.

Frankly I'm disappointed about the ghost. It was fun talking to Lili and Sam about it, being a detective, letting my imagination go wild. And hadn't Gran herself said there might be a ghost?

But in a bigger way, I'm relieved. No more lying in bed at night getting spooked every time the wind picks up, every time I hear a jingle-jangle, every time a lime falls off a tree.

"We still want to know what was in Veronica's letter," says Lili.

Angela sighs. "After the ceremony tonight I'm burning it. But I suppose she wouldn't mind terribly if you read it. You might as well know the whole truth."

The whole truth? I've got goose bumps again. A new mystery!

My mind races as I follow Angela and Lili back into the altar room. Was Veronica murdered? Did she murder her father? What horrible secret is folded up in that note?

# 24

## No Answers

When we get to the altar the letter is gone! Angela looks around the roomful of people, aghast. Then I spot Gran. She's nodding to me, holding a piece of paper in her hand. She scoots through the crowd toward us.

"Is this what you're looking for?" she whispers. "I saw you two looking at this letter. It blew off the altar and I picked it up." She passes it to Lili, who reads it in English to me.

```
14 marzo

Dear Father,

I am disowning you as my father as of
this date. You have no further right to
call me daughter, to treat me as a
daughter, to ever again mention my name.

I see it is too late for you to admit
the truth. Was your entire life about
nothing but money? Did I mean nothing to
you? Did life itself mean nothing to you?
```

Those poor people—how many of them are
dead because of you? And when you die,
will their blood be on my hands, too?

You are truly a coyote in every sense of
the word. I will not miss you.

v.

I am stunned.

What did Veronica mean by "how many are dead
because of you?" What people died? And...how?

"You see why I was so afraid that night?" whispers
Angela. "It scares me again now."

It's true. She's shaking. "I have to go," she says. "You
can keep the letter."

After Angela disappears quickly into the crowd, Lili
and I look at Gran, hoping she has answers. But she looks
as perplexed as the two of us.

"So what happened to Veronica?" I ask. "Do you think
she killed herself?"

"Maybe she just went back to wherever she came from,"
Lili suggests.

"We may never know," says Gran, shaking her head.
"But I have a feeling this isn't over yet. In the meantime,
we've certainly had our Day of the Dead ghostbusting
adventure, haven't we? I suggest that you two leave well
enough alone. Maybe this is one mystery that should be
left unsolved."

Lili looks at me. Then she takes a last look at the letter
and tears it into tiny bits. She puts her arm in mine and

we walk up to the altar together. She drops the scraps of paper into the incense. Together we watch them burn.

"Let's say good-bye to pain and sadness," she whispers. "And to any spirits who are still wandering because they are sad and in pain."

I say good-bye to Veronica, but I'm still thinking about her later when we drink our apple cider with the Sanchez family in our gremlin-lit garden.

"In the letter Veronica called her father a coyote," I say to Lili. "Does that mean migrant workers paid him to sneak them across the border?"

"Who knows?" says Lili, shrugging. "In Mexico a coyote is also what you call a person you can't trust."

I still can't stop thinking about Veronica the next night, on the official Day of the Dead, when we sit in the cemetery at the graves of Lili's grandparents and great-grandparents. Señora Sanchez is talking to the *chicos* about how plants die but new life sprouts from their seeds. How people die but they leave behind new life in the form of children and grandchildren.

"Do you think Veronica had children of her own who will be nothing like her father?" I whisper.

"Maybe," Lili says. "Like your grandmother said, we'll probably never know."

I'm still thinking about Veronica when Lili and I dance like jaguars in front of the church on November 20, *el Día de la Revolución*. We dance the sacred dance I learned in Señorita Murillo's class. When I start to move that morning, I feel shy, even though I'm only one of about two hundred other jaguars.

But by the time I dance again later in the day, I am finally able to feel the beat in my bloodstream. DUM da da da, DUM da da da goes the rhythm of the drums. My feet stamp along with it. I forget about making mistakes. I let go of trying to find answers about Veronica and her father. I feel bold and ferocious.

As Señorita Murillo would say, I dance the dance.

# 25

# Gibberish

"Your father is going to Colorado," my mom tells me on the phone that night. I'm sore from my daylong jaguar dance. I'm standing in the kitchen in a furry spotted toga with rattles on my ankles and teeth hanging around my neck.

"Big deal. I hope he has a great time," I say. "It's about time he took a vacation." Why should I care? I don't.

"No, Hayley. He's moving. He found a new job in Denver." She's trying to sound upbeat, but it's not fooling me. "He says it's just for a while."

Denver? Someplace far from Kalamazoo and far from San Miguel, too? My heart, which felt so courageous all day dancing, suddenly turns weak and achy. When will I ever see my dad again? I'd kind of imagined him moving closer. Like back inside our house.

"Is he planning to call and tell me himself?" I ask Mom.

"Well, I really don't know, honey," she answers. "I'm sorry."

I hang up, furious at my father. Hello, I'm your kid, remember? You used to call me your little squirrel. You said you were so happy I was born. We were a *family*. What happened to all that?

When I was little, my dad played with me a lot. I think. Okay, maybe I *wanted* him to play with me. So I've pretended, in my head, that we had lots of fun together. Truth is, I hardly ever do anything fun with my dad. It's all: "How's school? Working hard? Room tidy? Homework done?"

He has no idea who I am now that I'm not a little squirrel kid anymore. He gets distracted by work...and traveling for work, and staying late at the office to work, and spouting off about how important his work is.

But I don't really want to think about Dad and Denver any more right now. I can't do anything about all this anyway. So I decide to check up on other, more miserable lives. I'm going to spy on Señora Bruja next door.

The best way to do this is by standing on my tippy-toes in the shower, peeking out the round bathroom window, where she can't see me.

She's out there in the dark with her menagerie, dressed in overalls with a flowered shawl tied around her head and shoulders. She's got a flashlight in her hand and she's checking inside one of the piggies' mouths. She's chatting to him in a singsong voice. Maybe he has a toothache.

It's strange how some people love their animals and hate their neighbors. Couldn't she at least answer the door when I bring her a present? Couldn't she have called a little *gracias* over the wall?

Anger boils up in my heart and shoots through my veins like fireworks. Why am I so raging mad? It can't be only because of the lonely *bruja* next door.

I'm mad because Pulga's dad never came home the way he promised.

I'm mad because Lili's dad *can't* come home.

I'm mad because my mom is so miserable. I want her to see that even people who have nothing can be happy.

I'm mad because my stupid father is moving to Denver. Does he think he'll find something or someone there better than me and Mom? Who could be better than me and Mom?

My cell phone rings again. I step into the bedroom to get it.

Guess who? My dad. Calling for the first time since I've been here.

He's talking really fast.

He tells me about Colorado. "It's for the best, Hayley, and it doesn't mean I don't love you," he says.

I feel like he's rehearsed this. There's not one speck of emotion coming through. I want to scream at him. Scream like a wild jaguar with long, sharp teeth.

"How nice for you," I say.

My dad ignores my sarcasm. He never listens to anything he chooses not to hear.

"Hey, maybe I'll come down to Mexico for Christmas. I'm not sure if I can take the time off work, but I could try," he says. "New job, you know?"

What's with all his fake cheeriness? This fast-talking gibberish? I hate it. I need something *real* to hold on to right now.

"Right. Whatever. Well, I've got to go, Dad."

I'm glad that when I get off the phone Gran comes to put her arm around my furry jaguar toga.

"I'm sorry, *tesoro,*" she says.

"Me, too," I say.

"Did I ever tell you about the dried-up fish eggs?" Gran asks.

Oh, just what I want to discuss right now. Shriveled fish ova!

"Sometimes the rivers here in Mexico dry up," she continues. "The fish die and the eggs they laid just sit for years. When the rains come and the water flows back to the river, the eggs come alive and hatch. It's like the seeds under the frozen winter soil—"

"What are you saying, Gran?" I snap, pulling away from her. I know I sound cranky and rude. But I'm tired of being such a good girl all the time. I don't want to hear about seeds sprouting and fish hatching and all that garbage.

"Right now everything looks dead, but with some time and TLC, a new beginning always comes," Gran says.

While she talks I look at my spotted jaguar hands, not Gran's face, and I can't listen to another word about new life. At this moment I have to go throw up. I rush past her into the bathroom. Afterward I don't go back in where she is. I go out to my chicken coop for sanctuary. I yank off my Margarita's Sanctuary (No *Fantasmas* Allowed!) sign and chuck it into the compost.

Here I am in the middle of Mexico. I don't belong here. I'm pretending to be someone else, Margarita with her mango hair. And a ferocious jaguar face. What a joke! It's like I'm living someone else's life. That would be fine if I were an actress in a movie, speaking of which, *never* happened. It probably never will.

Promises. Promises. I'm so sick of promises.

I pick up a paintbrush and squeeze out some paints. I paint the face of a lonely squirrel-colored sheep under a pale moon. I give it luna moth–green eyes and make the mouth exactly like my own. A self-portrait.

I sit and stare at it. What do I have to go home to? Do I even have a home at all? My family is in pieces—Chicago, Denver, San Miguel. It's not as if my parents have gotten along that well the last few years. But I guess I didn't want to think it would get this bad. It's easier just to pretend everything is going to be fine.

I hate the truth. Okay, I hate *this* truth.

I start painting a garden of daffodils behind my sheep. They're bending down, heavy snow on their delicate little heads. I already know what to name this when I'm done: *Lost Sheep Under Lone Moon with Daffodils.*

Then I scrounge around for the little silver heart Gran mailed to me in Kalamazoo. My *milagro.* My hope for a miracle. I put some glue on the back and slam it onto the sheep's neck, hard.

# 26
# Take One! Take Two! Take Twelve!

Just two days after my jaguar dance, at exactly four o'clock in the morning, my alarm starts screeching. Normally waking at that hour would be enough to turn me into a cranky little witch for the whole day. But today is filming day! Me, Lili, and Alonzo Luna! I leap out of bed and make a beeline to go wash my face.

One of those little miracles I was waiting for has finally come through, and the timing is perfect! I mean, they were supposed to shoot this movie before school started. It turns out that the director had dropped the scenes with the San Miguel extras. At the last minute he changed his mind, and Jorge called us all in a frenzy. They have to shoot immediately, because the release date is set for December.

I have to meet Lili in twenty minutes and get a cab to the hotel where a bus is waiting to take us to Querétaro, the town where we're filming.

Because the movie people want my hair wavy I slept in big rollers all night, which is major torture. So now I get to walk around with an alien head until I arrive on the set, where they'll unroll me.

Gran is up calling a cab and making me drink a glass of juice before I leave.

"Gran, they feed you on the set," I snap.

What's happening to me? I used to drink what I was told to drink, and not complain. Ever since my dad called, I've been in a very bad mood.

"Quit acting like a sassy diva and just drink your juice," says Gran, talking like a sassy diva herself.

When the cab arrives, Gran hops in with us.

"You don't need to come," I tell her. "You'll have to make this trip again in a couple of hours."

Gran and Señora Sanchez are in a scene called "Opera House," not the scene with me and Lili. Later this morning they're headed for Guanajuato to film up in a mountain town that has a colonial opera house from the 1800s. They get to wear tiaras and long gloves and ornate gowns like theatergoers wore back then.

"Oh yes I *do* need to come," Gran tells me. "You betcha. It's four in the morning, and you are two *señoritas bonitas* traveling alone."

I guess I should feel complimented.

Lili's cousin Manuel will be meeting us in Querétaro to follow us around all day to make sure we're safe. Then he's bringing us home.

"Call me from your cell when you're done filming," Gran says as we board the extras' bus. "Break a leg, my little *chicas!*"

"You too, Gran!" I holler back.

"What?" asks Lili.

"You can explain the weirdness of the English language

137

to Lili on your trip," says Gran, blowing us little kisses. It *is* a weird expression, isn't it? Break a leg. There's no translation in Spanish, except *¡Buena suerte!* Good luck!

An hour later a harried-looking assistant is herding Lili and me and the other extras through the streets of Querétaro and into a building transformed to handle catering, makeup, costumes, and hair.

The staff starts primping us. A beautician takes out my rollers and piles my hair up into a complicated pouf, twirling little tendrils around my face and neck. Lili is next to me, and her ponytail has been transformed into an elegant French twist. Then the beauticians set our velvet hats on our heads and pin them just so.

Next we move to the makeup room, where we get powdered faces, rosy cheeks, and red lipstick.

"No eyes!" the makeup boss calls, walking around and checking out our faces. "Just lips and cheeks!" It means they won't put any eye shadow or mascara on us. I guess since we're extras, we can't be too stunning. We don't want to upstage Alonzo.

Some of the extras are acting pushy. They squeeze in line to be first to get their hair done. One is complaining about the color of her lipstick.

"Like anyone cares," I whisper to Lili. She shakes her head, amazed at their behavior.

*"Loca,"* she says.

We ignore the crazies and their griping. We're here to have fun, and we're soaking up every minute of it.

Finally we get to wardrobe. The costume director, who today chose to wear purple patent leather pants instead of his dining room drapes, pins my cameo on my lace collar.

*"Perfecto,* darling," he tells me, pinching my cheek. "Now, go, go, go!"

Lili and I hurry out onto the street where they're getting ready to film. We're standing taller, walking more gracefully, and definitely feeling five years older just because of how fabulous we look. We stand behind the cameras and wait with a hundred other extras.

We wait. And we wait. Our feet start aching. Then we wait some more. Every minute we're both watching to catch a glimpse of Alonzo, although we don't say that out loud. It would be totally immature and unprofessional.

We wait for *five hours* while they set up cameras and lights. Finally they tell us to take a break and go eat something. We head back into the extras building, and just as we sit down for some juice and quesadillas, a woman comes in screaming.

"Places, extras! We're rolling!" she hollers, like there's a fire someplace.

Sometimes I load too much paint on my brush and it leaves a big glob on my canvas. It looks like this woman had the same problem with her glittery blue eye shadow this morning.

"Back on the set!" she yells.

The whole room clears out onto the street, and they pair up us extras to do the scene. Lili and I walk arm in arm. We're pedestrians strolling along in the summer of 1914. The crew has changed all the Mexican store windows to make it look like old-time New York. There's a deli with fake hams and sausages and a bookstore full of English books and a clothing shop with turn-of-the-century American clothes.

The assistant directors keep putting up their hands to signal us to walk slower, slower. As the cameras roll, we walk and walk and walk. We check out the faces of the people we pass in case one is Alonzo.

"Cut!" yells the director. We do it again. Walk, walk, walk.

"Cut!" he hollers. We do it again. In fact, we do it ten more times. Twelve more times.

"It's a wrap!" he finally calls.

It's three hours later, the sun is setting, and my feet are blistered and screaming.

Now Jorge, the casting director, comes around, telling the extras that half of us can stay to do a second scene, which is supposed to be the winter of 1914, still in New York. Lili and I discuss whether we want to stay. Our feet are killing us. But...who knows? Maybe Alonzo will show up for the next scene!

"You'll need to wear coats this time," Jorge continues. "We're making snow." Snow? In the middle of Mexico?

Suddenly the diva in me surfaces. Hello? I'm from Michigan. I can totally do that snow scene! Who cares how tired I am? Lili also wants to stay since she's never seen snow in her whole life, even if it *is* fake. We start hopping around again like silly little jumping beans.

Jorge nods. "Okay, you two. You're in," he says.

They haul the snow machines to the set as we head inside for dinner.

"So do you think Alonzo will show up for this scene?" Lili asks one of the crew members.

"*¿Quién sabe?*" he says, as if it's not really important. He doesn't know? What's wrong with him?

"Places!" hollers the woman with the blobby blue eyes about an hour later. We hurry out to stand around again. The purple-pants costume director passes around 1914-style coats for us to wear. When we put them on we all start sweating, since we're really in Mexico and it's about eighty degrees.

The makeup people stroll around with blush and lipstick in their fanny packs. They pink up our cheeks and refresh our lips. They have a lot of powdering to do on all our shiny, sweaty extras faces.

It's midnight when the shooting finally starts. Yep, I said midnight. We're walking again, being pedestrians, but this time we have to pretend to shiver as we duck the falling snow.

"It's a wrap!" the director finally calls. By now it's one-thirty A.M. and I'm still spying around for Alonzo.

No luck.

Manuel gets me and Lili back home safe and sound.

I limp back into the *casita* just before three A.M. I know my red lips are smudged and my hair is all straggly. Gran is snuggled in her comfy chair waiting for me. The first thing out of her mouth is:

"He's even more handsome in real life."

"Who?" I ask, hoping she's not referring to whom I think she's referring.

"Alonzo Luna," she says dreamily. "He was in our opera house scene today. And he's quite the gentleman. He called me *abuelita*. He even signed this for me."

I collapse on the couch, seething with envy. Gran winks and tosses me the opera playbill she was holding in the scene. Neatly written across the bottom were these words:

*Para Hayley, a True Tesoro—*
*With All Best Wishes,*
*Alonzo Luna*

# 27
## The Dads

Well, it looks like San Miguel's fall fiestas are finally finished. I guess you could say the party is over—until Christmas, that is. Up in Michigan the harvest season is over, too. All the blueberries and grapes and apples and pumpkins are picked, and the snow is starting to fall.

The bad news is that the dads still haven't been paid. We know they're eating, thanks to the money from the Secret Giver. But they can't come home. They don't have enough bus money.

"We can't worry about the men without green cards anymore," I tell Lili. "We can't worry about anything but getting those dads home."

"But what can we do?" asks Lili.

I talked it over with Gran.

"Can't we just send them the money they need?" I asked her.

"But then that boss will get away with this scot-free," Gran pointed out. "He'll just keep doing it again and again to more migrant workers."

Gran doesn't think we can just hire a lawyer to fix everything, either.

"I'd like nothing more than to be a hero and go box that *dueño's* ears until he pays those dads what he owes them," Gran said. "But there are lots of legal issues involved when you're talking about migrant workers and the U.S. and Mexico."

Don't those employers know what they're doing to the Sanchez family? Or worse, do they know, but they just don't care? I'm pacing back and forth clutching Farley in my arms.

Think! I tell Farley. We need a solution here! I'm getting like Gran now, talking to a stuffed frog the way she talks to flowers and butterflies. Or the way *la Bruja* talks to pigs.

I watch the town go to bed. Lights off here, lights off there, and now the *Parroquia* goes dark.

Think!

Then I hear it. That same tinkle-jingle-jangle I heard the night before Lili's family found the money in the blank envelope.

It's the Secret Giver.

I look out the window. There's a figure slipping past our front door, its faint shadow floating on the wall beyond. At least I know it's not a ghost.

I slide into my slippers, and with Farley in my arms I tiptoe down the steps and past Gran, who has dozed off with her book. I slip out, creep past the garden to the outer wall, and peek through the little round window in the street door.

I hear the jingle-jangle again. My jaw clenches. Sure enough, the jingling stops at the Sanchez house. I watch as the shadow starts its way back up the street, toward our *casita*.

The only light on the street is from the moon, so I can barely see anything but a silhouette. My heart skips a beat. It's coming closer. I feel a tickle on my leg and look down to see the biggest, hairiest spider I've ever seen in my life.

I let out a scream and hit it with poor innocent Farley. The spider skitters up the wall. By the time I look back out the porthole, nobody is in sight.

# 28

# Tres Ghostbusters

At dawn there's a big commotion out on the street. But for once it's not fireworks. It's people. Somebody's shouting that Paco has a bike. Is it his birthday? No. And it's certainly not Christmas.

I scramble downstairs and out the door to see what's happening.

"For weeks Paco has wanted to help the family out by delivering sandwiches. But he needed a bike for his deliveries," says Lili, who's beaming with excitement. "And here it is! Somebody left it at the door last night!"

"It was an angel!" cries Señora Sanchez. "A true angel!"

I don't think so. An angel wouldn't cast a shadow or make jingly sounds. As I think of it now, that jingle-jangle noise was very familiar. Like something I heard in a dream. Or at home...

Gran? No. Now I know Gran can't be the Secret Giver. She was sleeping when I snuck down last night. And besides, where would she have hidden a bike without me seeing it?

The neighbors on Parakeet Street and passersby on their way to work smile as Paco tries out his bike. It's not new. But Paco doesn't care. It's shiny, the tires are good, and it works. The cobblestones are very bumpy, so he's having a hard time keeping the wheels straight. But he's off delivering his sandwiches by noon.

Lili comes over to help me finish up something important. After Day of the Dead we decided that until all Veronica's files are deleted, she's not completely free to be gone.

One last time we go back through the diary, and I don't like reading it anymore. Neither does Lili. It's more of a task now, like homework or something.

Veronica should have seen she wasn't like her dad. Whatever he did, it was his fault. Not hers. I'm hoping she changed into a whole new person and came out flying.

Like Gran says, making yourself happy, that's something we each have to do for ourselves.

I delete the trash, all of it, with one simple click.

It's gone. Go fly now, Veronica. Wherever you are, be happy. *Vaya con Dios.*

"How sad," I say, shaking my head.

"Yes," Lili agrees. "Because of her father, Veronica left a lot of negative energy around her."

"Why don't you two do something positive on that computer and change all that negative energy?" Gran asks.

Lili and I jump a mile.

"Gran!" I holler. "You could let us know when you're standing right behind us, for Pete's sake."

"Oh, sorry, girls," she says. "I was just going to sit out here and work on my investigation a bit."

"What are you investigating?" Lili asks.

"Oh, you'll find out soon enough," says Gran mysteriously. She has so many secrets. I'm just glad hers are the good kind.

Lili's face lights up. "An investigation..." she repeats. "I'm getting an idea."

"What?" I ask.

Lili looks off to the sky as if she's mulling something over. I stay quiet, giving her space to think.

"Yes!" she says finally. "I know how to use this computer in a better way."

"Tell me," I say.

"I'll write a letter to the newspapers in Michigan! I want them to know what is happening at the farm. Maybe someone important will want to investigate."

"What a great idea," I say, scooting off the chair so Lili can take over the computer. "There must be people back home who want to know that migrant workers aren't being treated fairly."

"You write it, and we'll help you with the English," Gran volunteers.

Lili sits down and starts typing.

While she's busy, I get a brainstorm, too.

"Gran, where's that picture you took of the Sanchez family at the kitchen table the night of the Farewell Fiesta?" I ask.

"In the drawer behind Pablo, I think," she says.

"Pablo? Oh yeah, the polka-dot rooster." I dash inside and get the photo.

"Do you want to read what I wrote?" Lili asks when she's done.

"Of course," Gran says. "Print it out and I'll check the spelling."

I scan the photo into the computer as Gran reads Lili's letter out loud.

Dear Everybody,

My dad is working in Michigan with a green card and he is in trouble. He and my Uncle Cristóbal and my Uncle Luis have been working on a farm at Vineyard Creek since August. Now it is November and they still have not been paid for their work. They are living in tiny shacks and hardly have enough food to eat. Meanwhile our families here in Mexico are hungry.

Do you remember when you had that early snow in Michigan on October 1st? My dad worked from four A.M. until two A.M.— almost twenty-four hours straight—to save the whole pumpkin crop. The farmer wrote down that my dad was paid $425 that week. But really the farm boss only gave him and my uncles each $39. After they bought food it was not enough to even pool together to go to the doctor when Uncle Luis got sick from overworking.

That was just one example of how they are treated. There are lots more.

```
    All they want to do is get paid for
the work they have done and come home.
We miss them. I don't know what to do,
since I live in Mexico. I am hoping
someone in Michigan knows. Please help.

                    Sincerely,
                    Liliana Olvera Sanchez
```

Gran adds our e-mail and phone number at the bottom, in case people want to contact Lili. We look up e-mail addresses for five newspapers. We attach the photograph of the Sanchez family sitting at the kitchen table with the Virgin of Guadalupe all red and green and twinkly on the wall behind them.

Lili hits Send. It's gone.

"It's like sending a message in a bottle," Gran says.

*"Perfecto!"* I say.

"I hope they print it and somebody reads it," says Lili.

I hope somebody cares enough to do something, I think.

# 29
# The Whole Truth and Nothing but the Truth

Dad is divorcing Mom. I can't believe it. I also can't believe that my mom actually sounds relieved. "Are you okay, Hayley?" my mom asks.

"Yes," I say. Then I say good-bye and hang up the phone.

How can I be okay? And besides, what if I'm not? Would that change things?

Even with my dad in Colorado and my mom starting a new career, I didn't think it would happen. I tried to tell myself it could happen. But in a secret place deep inside me, I really thought he'd come back to us.

"I gave up shams a long time ago," says Gran quietly.

I jump and swing around to see Gran in the doorway of my sanctuary. She's brought a tray. There's *Abuelita* cocoa with a pink marshmallow on top for each of us. And cheese puffs with her spicy mango salsa.

I open my mouth to ask her what she means about shams and instead of words, sobs start coming out. I close my mouth hard, trying to stop. I don't want to cry.

"Go ahead, *tesoro*," says Gran. "A little salt in the *Abuelita* won't hurt the taste." I can't stop, so I sit down to steady myself. My cocoa cup is shaking in my hands. The warmth feels good, and the chocolate smells like Gran to me, and I just shake and cry into my hot chocolate. The tears are steaming hot with anger.

"He left," I blurt between sobs. "He left us."

"I know," says Gran quietly. She sits on the chair beside me, just letting me cry.

"The daffodils," I whimper. "She's never...he'll never..."

"I know, sweetie," whispers Gran.

I don't know how long I sit there gasping and sobbing, but finally I take a breath and I feel my body relax and get softer. Finally I look up at Gran. What would I do without her?

"Why?" I ask. Gran reaches over and pushes a curl of hair from my eyes.

"Your mom married a man who didn't allow her to be who she was. Her true self," she says. "Now I'm not saying she married the wrong man. After all, you're a gift from that marriage, and nothing is more right than you."

Her words are making me cry all over again. Who's right? I want to ask. Where's the truth? Is it Mom's truth? Or Dad's truth?

"Your dad wanted a woman who could make him look good," she continues. "Do things his way. Hobnob at those conventions he thinks are so almighty important."

I know that's true.

"Your dad is what I would call a conformist. He conforms to the Rule of the Joneses. Nobody really knows who those Joneses are—they're invisible people who make invisible laws."

She pauses to crunch on a salsa-dipped cheese puff. "I guess those Joneses think everybody should be more like ordinary ketchup than sweet and spicy mango salsa."

"That's Dad, all right," I murmur. Gran nods.

"But some people have to always keep up with those invisible Joneses. Pull the wildflowers from the lawn. Make your house a showplace, not a home. Dress your kids like the neighbors' kids. Get the job with the important title, even if you hate it. Don't let anybody know if you're going through a tough time because they'll think you're weak and gossip about you."

I quietly sip my cocoa. I know exactly what she's saying.

"If you break the Rules of the Joneses," Gran continues, "you might not get invited to the right parties or get the promotion you want so you can make more money to keep up with the Joneses. A vicious circle. What a lot of hooey! But that's what your dad wants, sweetie.

"Which brings us to the opposite rule, the one I like to live by: Live and let live. What makes us think we can tell anybody else how to live his life? It's nonsense. Don't think for a minute you can change your dad. Or your mom either, for that matter. The only person you can—"

"Change is me," I butt in. I heard it in therapy a thousand and seventeen times. I start crying again. I'm sad because I've always wished I could change Mom and Dad and everybody else who isn't happy. But I can't.

"I know this is a hurting time for you, Hayley Cakes. But the sooner you see that your mom will heal, and you'll heal, and your dad will be fine living his own life his way, the better. It's not tragic. It just *is*."

I sigh and pick up a paintbrush, thinking maybe it will make me feel better to paint something, even in the dark. Then I set the brush back down.

"I wish I could paint right now," I tell Gran. "But I can't." All I can do is sit in my chicken sanctuary and cry. I'm crying like a faucet that keeps getting turned off and on, on and off. I don't know if I could totally turn it off if I tried.

"Sometimes it's good to paint your little heart out," says Gran. "And sometimes it's better to cry."

She's right. She kneels next to my chair and wraps her arms around me. I sob all over her Virgin of Guadalupe caftan. I'm crying because there won't be any more Christmases with me and Mom and Dad being all together. Because there won't be any more family camping trips in the summertime. And because something happened that I didn't want to happen.

"Our family died," I say then.

That makes me just start sobbing more. I know it's like Day of the Dead, when everything dies and then just when you think it's all over, new shoots come peeking through the ground. And life starts again in a whole new way.

Maybe something new and secret has already started in me. I just don't know what it is yet. I can't feel it. Right now, all I feel is loss.

# 30
# Lights, Camera, Action!

Just as my swollen eyes start to recover from two days of crying and I'm feeling a little calmer, everything explodes.

The phone rings all the time. E-mails pour in.

"How can we help?" people are asking.

They've read Lili's letter in the newspapers. Señora Sanchez and Lili are dashing over to our *casita* several times a day, huddling around the computer with me to see the notes coming in. People we don't even know want to help them! But all this doesn't seem to surprise the Sanchezes. In Mexico this sort of helping each other is a normal part of everyday life.

In Kalamazoo Sam's getting involved, too. We're talking on the phone every day.

"I'll foot the phone bill," Gran says. "It's my contribution to the Dad Cause."

Sam is all excited when I call her today. "I just sent you a front-page article from the Kalamazoo paper! They're doing a whole series on the migrant workers!"

"No kidding?" I say.

"It all started with Lili's letter to the editor," she says.

"It's fantastic! They sent attorneys and photographers and journalists out to Vineyard Creek..." She's talking so fast I can barely keep up. "Go check your e-mail and call me back!"

When I open my e-mail I can't believe what I see. The front-page headline is all about the migrant workers. The article starts like this:

### BROKEN PROMISES
### FARMWORKERS LIVE IN MISERY

Juan Sanchez's journey began 2,100 miles away, in the town of San Miguel de Allende, Guanajuato, Mexico, where he was not earning enough money to feed his family of five children. He and his brothers had worked as farmhands in the U.S. before, but this time was different. They heard that good wages could be earned at farms here in rural Michigan, and they contracted with crew boss Charles Vasquez, an intermediary between laborers and local farmers.

"We were told we'd receive honest pay for an honest day's work," Sanchez told this reporter. The brothers, green cards in hand, paid $325 each to travel north by bus to Michigan in August. When they arrived, they were hired and given a loan of $25 each for food until they received their first week's pay.

The article said that the farm boss didn't pay them for their work but kept lending them food money every week, charging them whopping interest on the loans. They had to pay back twice as much as they borrowed.

It's incredible. The e-mails are coming in so fast we can't keep up with them.

A Mexican American man whose father was a migrant worker and who owns a motel in Michigan offered to put the dads up in his motel for free until they can go home.

A big-time Detroit lawyer wants to represent the dads in court pro bono.

"What's pro bono?" I ask Gran.

"It means he'll do it for free!" says Gran.

Excellent!

And get this: Gran just heard that the owner of a San Miguel restaurant is going to host a fancy benefit showing of the Alonzo Luna movie. He plans to give all profits to the families of the migrant workers.

As soon as Gran tells me the good news, I race out the door and over to Lili's.

"The movie's coming out!" I yell. "And someone is throwing a big premiere party here in San Miguel! Even better, all the money will go to the migrant workers!"

"Fantastic!" says Lili. "Are we invited?"

"Of course!" I say. "We're the famous extras!"

And here's the best volunteer offer we've had so far—for me, anyway. My mom called. She and Sam's mom have decided to start calling organizations in Michigan who might be able to help not just the San Miguel dads, but other migrant workers who are stuck in the same situation.

"What do you think?" Mom asks me.

"I think I love you a whole bunch, Mom," I tell her.

At this moment I feel right at the center of everything, just like San Miguel is right in the middle of Mexico. Who ever knew that in the middle of nowhere somehow I'd feel smack-dab where I belong?

# 31
## Famous Feet

**Y**esterday a fancy lavender envelope addressed in silver pen came for Gran and me in the mail. Inside was an invitation from that ritzy hotel in the center of town:

*You are invited to be our guest*
*At the local television premiere of*
*BORDER CROSSINGS*
*Starring Alonzo Luna*
*and the cast of extras from San Miguel*
*Seven P.M. to midnight*
*Saturday, December 1*
*Drinks and Appetizers Provided*

*Please bring photos and souvenirs for our*
*Extras Bulletin Board*

What a fiesta this is going to be! We extras get to come free because we're part of the attraction. Everyone else in town will pay one hundred pesos and the profits will be sent to the migrant dads and their families.

We'll all wear fancy clothes, and some people will actually come in 1914 costumes like we wore in the movie. We hear that a few supporters are thinking of dressing as migrant workers in honor of the occasion.

Lili and I go shopping for elegant outfits at the *mercado*. The market is like a carnival, with bright tents stretching for blocks and blocks. You can buy anything your heart desires: herbs to cure your boils and ulcers, Mexican-style Barbies with platform shoes and glittery outfits, chickens, masks, sofas, tools, fruits and vegetables, and Señor Sanchez's birds, which Lili's brother César is selling while their dad is gone. There are also mounds and mounds of clothes—some new, some used, some vintage.

Lili finds a pale blue satin dress with a rhinestone belt and a slit up the side. I go for velvet pants, a silver silk top, and a feathery boa to toss over my shoulders. My whole outfit sets me back six bucks. Just to be clear, ordinarily we would not be seen dead in clothes like these. But it's our big Hollywood night, so we decide to be a little outrageous.

Hollywood! I remember Lili's little sister Isabel and how I promised to get her a souvenir from the film. I spot a long pink dress with a high neck and sequin flower designs woven through the fabric. Perfectly vintage.

"It looks like it came straight out of 1914, doesn't it?" I

ask Lili. "Let's get it for Isabel and invite her to the party. Gran will buy her a ticket for sure."

"She will love it!" exclaims Lili, hugging me.

My mom will be watching the movie at home with Samantha's family. Most of my class in Kalamazoo is going to watch, too. It's a TV movie, and since we're all in the same time zone, it runs at the same time in both countries. Mom and Sam will be calling my cell after it's over to discuss the new starlets—namely me and Lili and Gran.

At seven o'clock everybody starts arriving, decked out in fabulous clothes. The hotel has run a red carpet from the street to the entrance, and everyone's shooting pictures. A host in a black satin tuxedo gives each of us extras a flower at the door—a white rose. Spiffy waiters are dashing around with drinks and juices and spicy canapés on trays.

"¡Elegante!" whispers Lili.

You'd think it was the mini Oscars. We pin our movie souvenirs on the bulletin board around the glossy photo of Alonzo Luna in the middle. I must say, among the costume tags and photos, Gran's autographed opera bill takes the cake.

Just before nine P.M. we all go into a meeting room, which has been set up like a theater. There are candles on little round tables covered with white tablecloths. We take our seats. The music surges and the movie starts on a giant screen.

Lili and I are wriggling around, shoulders touching, so excited to see ourselves looking like we just stepped off the *Titanic!*

The film starts way out in the middle of a Mexican desert. A band of wild-looking *bandidos* are traveling with Alonzo Luna, and the camera zooms in on their faces.

"It's Bronco!" I holler. He's standing right in front of the camera holding a machete, his eyes squinting into the sun. His face is grimy and covered in dried blood.

"That's a fierce look on your face!" Lili's mom tells him. "And that makeup is so real!" I turn around to see that Bronco is at the table behind us. He's in boots, jeans, and a John Deere cap—I guess he's supposed to be a migrant worker from Michigan. He's looking pretty darned *guapo*.

I turn back to the movie and Bronco is still on camera. He looks ten years older on screen in his tall black boots and a red scarf tied around his head.

Pretty soon the movie switches to a winter street in 1914.

"That's our scene!" I announce to the people around us. Lili reaches over and holds my hand, Mexican *chica* style.

On the screen all the pedestrians are strolling along the shops on a New York street, and you'd never in a million years guess that it was filmed in Mexico. The snow is falling. The wind is blowing. Then the camera zooms in for close-ups. I squeeze Lili's hand.

But something's screwy. The camera's not shooting any faces. Just feet. Feet passing snowdrifts. Feet stepping in melted puddles. Feet waiting on curbs to cross the street. Men's feet. Children's feet. Ladies' feet.

"Look, Margarita! Those are our feet!" Lili shouts. "Your boots with the buttons! My green shoes!"

I try to act excited, but I'm mortified. All my friends in

Kalamazoo are glued to their TV sets watching for my face at this very moment, watching for my black velvet hat with the red curls peeking out. All they'll see is a pair of old-fashioned boots they won't even recognize.

"*¡Felicidades!*" I hear Bronco call from the table behind. "What great-looking feet!"

Just kill me now, I think. I want to crawl under my little theater table and then slither all the way home to my *casita.*

"I am sorry the director made a poor decision," Bronco says, tapping me on the shoulder. He continues in Spanish.

I have to ask Lili to translate. She quotes him. "The director did not realize the film would be a much bigger hit if he put your beautiful face in it." When I understand what he's said, I feel myself turn bright red. "Um, *gracias,*" I tell him. "I think."

I turn to Lili and whisper, "So much for our big careers as movie stars."

"There's still the summer scene, remember, Margarita?" says Lili. "Maybe we'll be in that one."

"Shhhh!" calls somebody up front. "We're missing some good stuff here!"

The film is moving at lightning speed. The extras are basically ignoring the story and even Alonzo Luna. We just want to examine every single frame to find extras from San Miguel in the background.

Finally we come to the colonial opera house scene. The camera sweeps past the chandeliers and carved balcony rails. It pans the audience watching from their red velvet seats and zooms in on...Gran and Señora Sanchez!

In the movie they're acting horrified at whatever is happening on the stage, their eyes huge, their gloved hands raised to their mouths. They look awesome!

"You're a natural, Susi!" calls one of Gran's friends.

"*¡Qué bella,* Maria!" someone hollers to Señora Sanchez. "You look beautiful!"

Gran and Lili's mom start elbowing each other, chuckling and getting a big kick out of their brush with fame. They're the stars of the night.

Then the movie is over. They must have cut our other scene. I guess I have to be satisfied that I have a pair of famous feet.

In the middle of the post-film party, Mom and Sam call my cell phone. They took a picture of Gran and Señora Sanchez right on the television screen. And Sam's excited when I explain that the young *bandido guapo* was none other than Bronco.

"But hey, we didn't see you!" they complain.

"How could you have missed me?" I say, in my best diva voice. "I was the one splashing through the snowy puddle in my high-heeled boots."

"Of course, sweetie," my mom tells me. "With feet like that, you're bound to be going places!"

# 32

# Noche Buena

The whole town is decorated to welcome baby Jesus. Bright lanterns—not just red and green, but every color—are strung from tree to tree in the *Jardín*. Live burros and lambs lie in the straw at the foot of the manger.

Every night for the past two weeks there's been a *posada,* a procession from house to house. Crowds carry candles up and down the cobblestone streets, following Mary and Joseph to the inns. They knock on doors, their lanterns in hand, singing a song that asks if they can stay for the night. People keep saying no until finally an innkeeper says yes and everyone crowds inside the house to celebrate. They have found a warm place for baby Jesus to be born.

Gran and I have been celebrating the season ourselves in a whole new way. The evergreens down here are pretty skimpy and stubby, so we decided to decorate the garden. Instead of just one Christmas tree, we have a whole Christmas garden!

We string twinkle lights on the avocado and lime trees. We hang shiny little tin ornaments all over the place.

Everything looks magical. The only thing missing is snow. But I figure I got my share on the movie set.

Then we invite Lili over for a gift-wrapping night.

"We have some special presents to give," Gran announces when Lili arrives. First she gives us both homemade eggnog, which Lili has never tasted. Lili has brought us Christmas tamales and a hot corn drink, called *atole,* with chocolate in it.

Gran proceeds to pull a bunch of surprises out of the cupboard: tiny boxes, bright tissue papers, shiny ribbons. Then come dog bones and birdseed and animal toys. Lili and I exchange perplexed looks and shrug.

"Gifts for Veronica," says Gran.

We don't get it. Are we doing another Day of the Dead altar or something?

"Veronica, who lives next door with all her animals," says Gran. It takes a minute for that to sink in.

"*¿La Bruja?*" Lili and I whisper together. "Veronica is *la Bruja?*"

"I think it's time everyone stopped calling her that," says Gran sharply. "She's a sweet woman who's had a hard life, that's all."

It turns out that Gran went to the courthouse to check the records of ownership for her house. By accident she discovered that the owner of the house next door had also owned our *casita* a few years back. Her father had died, and he passed the house on to her.

"Remember the man in the cowboy hat at the bar? The one who bought me a beer after the running of the bulls?" she asks. How could I forget?

"His name is Mario. He works at the courthouse," Gran continues. "I just happened to see him there the day I checked the records. He told me the whole story about Veronica and her father."

"Tell us, tell us!" Lili and I exclaim.

Veronica's father *was* a coyote. He charged $600, $700, sometimes as much as $1,000 to help illegal migrant workers cross the border. He had been born in San Miguel. So word got around he was the man to see if you wanted to sneak illegally up to the States to work. He was local, so everyone thought he could be trusted.

But somewhere along the line Veronica's father discovered he could make money more easily by cheating. He began taking the money and then deserting the men when it was time for the perilous crossing.

"A lot of those men had no alternative but to try to cross the Rio Grande by themselves. They had gotten all the way up to the border. They had spent all their money. Their families were counting on them. They ran or swam for it," says Gran sadly. I don't want to hear any more, but she continues.

"Mario says at least five San Miguel migrants died at the border. One of them was seventeen years old, another eighteen."

Lili's face is in her hands. I know what she's thinking—if things were different, if her father didn't have a green card, the same thing could have happened to him, to her uncles. I suddenly hate that old man as much as Veronica did. Maybe I've had a hard time with my own father, but at least he's not a *murderer!*

167

"Anyway," Gran goes on, "the coyote came back to San Miguel when he was diagnosed with cancer. He bought this house quietly and hid out so no one would recognize him. If he'd been found out, the locals might have killed him."

Now Gran starts cutting paper and ribbons and hands us little gifts to wrap.

"So when Veronica inherited this house, she didn't want to live with the horrible memories. But she wanted to stay in San Miguel. So she moved next door, leaving everything behind that could possibly remind her of her father."

"Including the computer," I say.

"Exactly," says Gran. "Later, through her lawyers, she sold the *casita* to me."

"It seems like she is still such an unhappy woman," says Lili.

"Yes, but there's not much we can do about that, is there?" Gran gives me a little smile.

"Nope," I say. "We can't make her happy. We can only make ourselves happy."

"But that doesn't mean that we can't brighten her Christmas a little. So let's have some *atole* and some eggnog and let's get wrapping!" says Gran. She reaches over and turns on Christmas music.

We work like elves, tucking and folding and tying bows while we sing along with the music. When we're done, we pile everything on Veronica's doorstep and ring the bell. We know she won't answer, at least not until we've left. She doesn't. The teeny gifts wrapped and tied in all different colors look magical to me. I think they'll look magical to Veronica, too.

Now it's *Noche Buena,* the "Good Night"—Christmas Eve.

I call home.

First I call my dad. Some woman answers, so I hang up. Maybe it's his housekeeper or something. Maybe he's having people over for Christmas Eve and a guest answered the phone. Or...face it, Hayley. It's his girlfriend and he has a whole new life without you. Without Mom.

Somehow realizing this doesn't hurt as much as I would have thought.

Then I call my mom. As her phone's ringing I look out my window at the ten-foot-tall poinsettias, bursting with red flowers. Here they're called *nochebuenas,* because they're always in full bloom on Christmas Eve.

Mom sounds genuinely happy. Warm. Like all her inside corners are toasty now. She's back home in Kalamazoo. And she's at school every day cooking up a storm. We sent her twelve presents from Mexico, one for each of the twelve days of Christmas, and she opens the first one—a soft shawl made from alpaca—while I'm on the line.

"I love it!" she says. "I miss you so much, sweetheart."

"I miss you, too, Mom," I tell her.

"So it's been six months," she says.

"Yep," I say.

"Are you ready to come home?"

I *am* home. For now, anyway, I think. Not forever. Just for now. "I'm thinking about finishing the school year here," I say.

I wait for my mom to say no.

But she doesn't. "Well, only if I can come visit San

Miguel for your birthday week," she says brightly. "And maybe again during my spring break. And only if you promise me you'll be back to stay in Kalamazoo when summer comes."

"I promise, Mom," I tell her. I can't believe it. She said yes! And she's coming to visit!

"Mom's coming to Mexico!" I shout to Gran. I haven't felt this great in a long time.

"Thanks, Mom. I love you," I say.

"Merry Christmas," she says. "I couldn't love you more, sweetie."

When I get off the phone I open my presents from Gran. First I get a pair of binoculars.

"For my bedroom observatory?" I ask.

"Maybe," Gran says. "Keep opening."

Next I get hiking boots. Then a new sketch pad. A bus ticket to the state of Michoacan.

"Am I going on an adventure?" I ask.

"We're going together!" Gran chirps. "We're going to the forest where the monarchs migrate for their winter vacation. I thought a New Year's trip into the butterfly forest would do us good."

"Just the two of us?" I ask.

"You betcha," says Gran. "You, me, and millions of monarchs!"

"I can't wait!" I say.

"They say that a single tree there can be covered with more than a hundred thousand butterflies," says Gran. "Then maybe, just maybe, we'll take a couple of days at an ocean resort for a good rest."

I can't wait to see more of Mexico.

"What a great present, Gran!" I exclaim, and I mean it.

Then I give Gran her present. It's a portrait of her in her straw hat surrounded by flowers and butterflies. I've pounded heart *milagros* into the yellow frame. Around the edges I've written "Little miracles are everywhere. You just have to look with your heart." I know Gran really likes it because her eyes are full of tears. She takes an old painting off the wall and hangs this one in its place.

At midnight Lili and her mom and brothers and sisters come over for a *Feliz Navidad* supper Gran and I cooked earlier in the day. I'm getting used to these late-night visits now. The trick is, you always have to take a siesta in the afternoon. Then you have the energy to stay up until two A.M. or even later.

"Close your eyes, Hayley," says Lili.

"Hayley?" I repeat. She never uses my real name.

"That's what the Michigan newspapers call you," Lili says with a big grin. "It's what your name was when you first came. It's a beautiful name. I'd keep it if I were you."

She puts her hands over my eyes so I can't see.

"*¡Ándale,* Ricardo! Hurry!" she calls to her little brother. I hear his footsteps coming toward me and feel him set a warm furry something in my arms. Lili takes her hands away and my eyes shoot open.

It's a kitty!

"Next winter, when the snow is falling in Kalamazoo, she will keep you cozy," says Lili. The whole family comes over to give me hugs one by one. I'm so happy!

I rub noses with the kitten, who is the most adorable

little thing I've ever seen. She has gray eyes and her fur is light, almost Dreamsicle orange. I lean my ear down next to her mouth, pretending like she's telling me a secret.

"She's whispering her name," I tell the *chicos*.

"*¿Cómo se llama?* What is her name?" they ask, their eyes wide.

"Pumpkin," I say. "She says her name is Pumpkin."

# 33
# Butterfly Whispers

It's New Year's Day and I'm standing with my mouth hanging open in the middle of the most unbelievable sight I've ever seen. Gran and I have hiked up the steep trail into the Michoacan forest, and the tree trunks and limbs are completely orange and black.

All of sudden you notice everything moving, shifting. You hear tiny rustling sounds—wings opening, closing, opening, closing.

The trees are covered with butterflies! I mean, totally *covered*. The trunks are butterflies. The limbs are butterflies. The leaves are butterflies. You have to be careful where you step because there are butterflies all over the ground soaking up water and nectar and sunshine.

Gran and I and the other hikers keep our voices low because we don't want to disturb this amazing thing that's going on.

"Your grandpa used to say if God had given me the choice between being a woman or being a butterfly," says Gran, "I would have fluttered away and he never would have seen me again."

"I'm glad you didn't," I whisper back. "Or I might never have happened."

"Oh, what a horrible thought!" Gran says, genuinely shocked at the idea.

As we stand and gaze and listen, thoughts pass through my mind like little whispers that float in and then leave, disappearing into the flickering forest.

I think about the dads. I'd like to tell you they all got home on Christmas Day with their arms full of presents—and that my dad was with them. And that everybody hugged and cried and stayed up all night laughing and talking and we had the best Christmas ever.

But that's not what happened. Things don't always happen like in the movies. They happen in their own time and sometimes they don't happen at all.

My dad didn't come for a holiday visit. He probably never will. But you already knew that.

It was December 28 when Mom called to tell us that the migrant dads were on their way.

"Samantha's mom and I went down to the bus depot ourselves to see them off," said Mom. "They'll be there in two days."

"Fantastic!" I wanted to climb through the phone and give her a big, warm Mexican hug.

"You're the best, Mom!" I told her.

Gran and Señora Sanchez sprang into action. Out came tables and chairs and streamers and lanterns and banners from every house on our block. Well, not *la Br*—I mean, Veronica's—but almost every house. Lili and I went shopping at the *mercado* for *piñatas* and "dad" presents, things like shoe polish and screwdrivers.

When they got off the bus at dawn on December 30 the dads looked thin and tired and completely happy. I just stood with my arm around Gran, watching all the moms and kids hug those dads. Behind them the sunrise was pink and I couldn't stop crying.

Now, standing here in the monarch forest, everything seems new. It's a new year for Mom, for Gran, and especially for me. Who knows what changes are in store?

I have a feeling about one person who's already started changing. I know who the Secret Giver is. You probably figured it out before I did, huh?

That familiar jingle-jangle is what I hear every morning coming from the zoo next door. On Christmas night I was on my tiptoes checking out what Veronica and her animals were doing to celebrate. She had found our presents and was happily sharing them with her menagerie.

Suddenly she looked straight up at my window and waved. The *milagros* on her wrist shook. It finally dawned on me where I'd heard that tinkly sound before. It's that *milagro* bracelet she wears every day, jingling and tinkling, shaking and jangling.

I waved and smiled. She smiled back. If Veronica has started to change, well, I figure anything's possible.

And I'm not telling a soul about her story. Her secret's safe with me.

A butterfly flutters down, landing on my shoulder.

"You know what they say?" Gran says. "St. Anthony Abad is the patron saint of animals in Mexico. They say he was so sensitive to the creatures of the earth that he could hear the whisper of a butterfly."

I listen for whispers. I'm getting an inkling of what I'll

paint next. I don't think it will be about dads. Like *la fantasma,* that story already feels old. I want to paint something new.

Maybe I'll paint the whole butterfly forest, which Gran says is flickering with over a hundred million monarchs right now.

Or maybe I'll paint a single tree full of butterflies soaking up the warm Mexican sun. Soaking up their companionship with each other. Soaking up life until it's time for them to fly back up north.

Or maybe I'll just paint one butterfly, the one on my shoulder. I imagine that I can hear it whispering in my ear. It's still only January, it whispers. It's still pretty cold up there in Michigan. There will be a time to leave this forest and head north.

But not quite yet. Right now this butterfly has a lot more soaking up to do.

## The End

**Linda Lowery** grew up in Chicago. From the age of seventeen, she has had a passion for traveling the world to get a feel for how other people live. She taught English in Athens, was a very good nanny to *bambinos* in Rome, a very bad cook in Florence, a travel agent in Honolulu, and an international flight attendant. She and her author/illustrator husband Richard Keep live in San Miguel de Allende, Guanajuato, Mexico, where they teach writing workshops. Their son Kris often visits, traveling and studying indigenous music. Linda loves to garden, and creates painted furniture with vibrantly colored jungle scenes. Purple jaguars, orange lizards, and green monkeys can often be found hiding in the red leaves.

A *New York Times* best-selling author, Linda has won many awards and honors for her multicultural fiction and nonfiction children's books. TRUTH AND SALSA is her first novel for Peachtree.

To learn more about Linda Lowery, please visit her website at *www.lindalowery.com*.